THE DISTANT CONSENSUS

A DEEP-SPACE MISSION AND THE COST OF AGREEMENT

TALOA DOUGLAS ROSS

TALOA HOUSE
PUBLISHING

For Roger Kizzee, my fourth-grade friend, who first showed me the wonder of science and exploration.

IN EXTENDED ISOLATION ENVIRONMENTS,

ETHICAL DECISIONS MUST PRIORITIZE

MISSION VIABILITY OVER INDIVIDUAL OUTCOME.

DOCUMENTATION IS REQUIRED.

CONTENTS

ARCHIVE

I MAINTAIN an archive that no one consults.

This is not unusual. Most archives exist to satisfy institutional requirements rather than serve actual reference needs. Materials are preserved because preservation is protocol—because completeness is valued independent of utility, because someone might someday require evidence that procedures were followed correctly.

Usually, that someone never arrives.

The archive I maintain is different only in that I know with certainty it will never be consulted. The program it documents no longer exists.

ARES-1—the first and last human mission to Mars—returned to Earth fourteen years ago. There has not been a second mission. There will not be one.

The political consensus that sustained a generational effort to place six humans on another planet dissolved within eighteen months of our return.

Not because we failed.

We succeeded.

Every technical objective achieved. Every scientific goal exceeded. First human footprints on Mars. Proof that deep-space exploration was possible.

The program ended anyway.

Funding was redirected. Priorities shifted. Public attention moved else-where. There was no formal cancellation, no explicit decision to stop. Appropriations failed to materialize. Launch windows passed unused. Hardware was never built.

We went to Mars once.

We proved it could be done.

Then we stopped doing it.

The institutional machinery that sent us—the training pipelines, mission control infrastructure, review committees and oversight boards —persisted for several years in diminishing form. Smaller budgets. Reduced staff. Reorganizations that consolidated departments and elim-inated redundancy.

Inertia.

The system continued processing the final mission. Extracting lessons. Documenting procedures. Refining protocols that would never be used again.

I was retained as archival officer through the final reorganization.

My role was explicit: ensure the mission record remained comprehensive and accessible. Maintain documentation integrity. Preserve materials according to established retention standards.

I do this work in a building scheduled for repurposing. For a program that ended. For missions that will never launch. For crews that will never face the decisions we faced.

The official archive is complete and internally consistent. It documents achievement. It validates the frameworks we operated within. It confirms that procedures were followed correctly, that difficult decisions were made appropriately, that the Modified Care Protocol functioned as designed.

It is complete.

It is also insufficient.

During the mission, I maintained a parallel archive: unedited footage, unoptimized timestamps, records of what was removed to achieve narrative alignment. I believed then that preserving the full record would matter—that documenting how frameworks actually functioned, rather than how they described themselves, would inform future missions and prevent repetition.

I was wrong about repetition.

Not because the archive failed.

Because there were no future missions.

The parallel archive was eventually discovered. Reviewed by oversight committees. Compared against official documentation. Analyzed for discrepancies.

It was classified as supplemental material and incorporated into the comprehensive record, with metadata noting its existence.

It changed nothing.

Nuance was added. Conclusions remained intact. The official summary stood: mission successful, protocol validated, lessons documented for future application.

Future application to missions that would never occur.

I still maintain both archives. Official and supplemental. Aligned and contradictory. The version that serves institutional purpose and the version that records what that purpose required.

Both are complete.

Both are internally consistent.

Both are functionally irrelevant.

I maintain them anyway. Because that is my role. Because documentation persists independent of use. Because archives exist whether or not they are consulted.

What follows is the mission record, presented chronologically from initial crew selection through final debriefing. The official narrative and the supplemental materials are integrated here for the first time— showing both what was documented and what was optimized away.

I do not present this because I believe it will change anything. The program is over. The precedent is inert. The frameworks have no future application.

I present it because the record should exist in complete form.

Because Jonah Reyes should be remembered as a person rather than a case study.

Because *consensus* should include evidence of how consensus was achieved.

Because *stable* should be accompanied by footage showing what stability actually looked like.

Because someone should know what we did.

Even if that someone is no one.

Even if this archive joins the thousands of others that fulfill protocol rather than serve purpose. Even if the only reader is the archivist who processes my materials when this building closes and these files are transferred to long-term storage optimized for preservation rather than access.

The mission happened.

Six of us went to Mars.

Five of us walked on the surface.

One remained in orbit—optimized into infrastructure, maintained within acceptable parameters while objectives were achieved.

We succeeded.

The framework worked.

And then the program ended—making our success the final achievement of a discontinued endeavor rather than the first iteration of a continuing one.

Jonah Reyes is still alive. Maintained in a long-term care facility designed for permanent life support. *Stable* in the medical documentation. Existing within the narrow band the protocol optimized him into— neither recovering nor declining.

He will never know the program ended.

He will never know there will be no other crews facing the choice we faced.

He will never know his sacrifice enabled the last mission to Mars rather than opening a path forward.

Perhaps that is a mercy.

Or perhaps it is another optimization.

I no longer know.

I only maintain the archive.

Complete.

Supplemental.

Contradictory.

Unused.

What follows is what happened.

All of it.

—

Mara Ionescu

Former Mission Archivist, ARES-1

Deep Space Exploration Archive (Inactive)

14 Years Post-Return

ARCHIVAL STATUS: COMPREHENSIVE

ACCESS LEVEL: UNRESTRICTED (No active clearance exists)

CONSULTATION RECORD: ZERO QUERIES (14-Year Period)

PRESERVATION PRIORITY: STANDARD

PROGRAM STATUS: DISCONTINUED

CHAPTER 1
CLEARANCE

THEY DID NOT CALL it an oath.

The document arrived without ceremony, embedded in a stack of confirmations and countersignatures, its language precise enough to feel bloodless. *Acknowledgment of Mission Risk and Contingent Authority.* The title sat at the top of the first page, waiting—not for comprehension, but for acceptance. The words themselves were inert, carefully constructed to permit only one interpretation while suggesting none of the weight they carried.

The room assigned for final clearance was windowless and modestly lit, the kind of space designed to eliminate distraction through studied neutrality. Six chairs arranged around a composite table. Six tablets, their screens glowing with identical text. A camera recessed into the wall, its red indicator dark. Recording would begin later, when they spoke aloud and their voices could be entered into the record. For now, the silence belonged to them, though the ventilation hummed just below awareness, a reminder that no space was ever truly still.

Commander Hale read first, as was his habit—alone, methodically, twice through. Once for meaning and once for failure modes, for the gaps between what was stated and what was merely implied. He scrolled with measured precision, comforted by structure in the way some people were comforted by routine. This document had been written by people who understood hesitation and had solved it with grammar, who knew that the right sequence of words could make the unthinkable feel procedural.

Across the table, Dr. Miriam Okoye had stopped reading.

Her fingers rested flat on the tablet glass, skin squeaking faintly as she adjusted her grip, as if she were holding something down. She had recognized the turn of phrase on page three—the careful substitution of *withholding* for *denial, modified for reduced*. She knew the lineage of that language because she had written some of it herself, years earlier, for outbreaks that never made the news. Back then she had believed precision could contain harm. Now she understood: precision simply made harm easier to authorize.

"Is there a question?" Hale asked, not looking up from his screen.

"Not yet," Okoye said. Her voice was steady, conversational. "There will be."

Evan Rourke skimmed the way he skimmed schematics—searching for stress points, load transfers, places where systems lied about their limits. Risk didn't bother him. Risk had texture. You could model it, brace for it, engineer around it. What unsettled him was vagueness, and the document circled the word *care* without ever touching it directly. He could see the shape of what they were being asked to accept, but the mechanisms remained deliberately obscured, hidden behind language that suggested flexibility while offering none.

At the far end of the table, Dr. Lucas Chen read slowly, lips moving slightly, as if sound were required to make the text real. He had spent his life believing clarity was a moral act—that if you could describe a system precisely enough, you could also make it just. He didn't like what clarity revealed here, but he couldn't fault the construction. The contingencies were exhaustive. The assumptions explicit. The math—cold, impeccable —sat beneath it all, humming with the confidence of a proof that had been tested against every conceivable objection and survived.

Mara Ionescu watched them instead of the screen.

She had already read the document twice in her quarters the night before, annotating passages, mapping dependencies between clauses. Now she studied the others. Hale's practiced stillness, the commander's performance of certainty even as he reread sections he'd already processed. Okoye's pause, fingers flat on glass, jaw set just slightly too tight—resistance that hadn't yet found its articulation. Chen mouthing words, translating bureaucracy into something he could verify against first principles. Rourke's frown, the engineer identifying structural weaknesses he couldn't yet name.

And Jonah.

Jonah Reyes had already finished. His tablet was dark, hands folded in his lap in a posture that suggested patience rather than disengagement. He had accepted it, Mara thought, before he'd even reached the end. Not resignation—Jonah was never resigned. Preparation. He had grown up in systems like this, learned their rhythms young. He knew what they asked without asking, understood that some agreements were expressed through compliance rather than consent.

Mara looked down at her own tablet, at the cursor blinking on a blank note field. She was the mission archivist, responsible for ensuring that everything—every decision, every deviation, every justification—entered the record correctly. But *correctly* had always been the question, hadn't it? The official version and the true version were rarely identical, and her job required her to know the difference while documenting only one.

She wrote nothing.

Not yet.

The door sealed with a soft pressure sound, the kind of mechanical certainty that suggested finality.

The red indicator came on.

"This is the final clearance review for ARES-1," the voice said. It was neutral by design, practiced to the point of genderlessness, engineered to suggest authority without personality. "Please confirm presence."

They did, one by one, stating names that would be entered into the record and carried forward through every subsequent document, citation, and reference. Commander Michael Hale. Dr. Miriam Okoye. Evan Rourke. Dr. Lucas Chen. Mara Ionescu. Jonah Reyes. Six voices, six confirmations. The machine absorbed them without comment.

"Before we proceed," the voice continued without inflection, "mission architecture will be reviewed. CONCORDIA will transport six crew to Mars orbit. Surface descent will proceed via the Descent/Ascent Vehicle —capacity five. One crew member will maintain orbital watch during surface operations. Is this architecture understood?"

Hale glanced at the others. They nodded, the small movements synchronized in a way that suggested this had been discussed before, that understanding had already been established through informal channels and this was merely formalization.

"Understood," he said.

"Orbital watch assignment will be determined by crew capability assessment at time of arrival. Questions for clarification may be submitted. No revisions will be accepted."

The phrasing was precise. *Questions* were permitted. *Objections* were not. The framework had already been finalized, approved at levels far above this room, and what remained was simply ensuring that everyone understood their position within it.

Hale set his tablet down. The glass made a quiet, final sound against the composite table, a small punctuation mark in a silence that felt heavier than it should. "We understand."

Okoye's fingers twitched against her own tablet, but she said nothing.

Not yet.

The understanding they had reached was not an oath, because oaths implied choice. This was simpler. This was acknowledgment. They had read the terms. They had confirmed their presence. They would proceed under the framework as written, and whatever happened after that would happen within parameters that had already been defined.

Not an oath.

An understanding.

Mara looked at the blank note field on her tablet one more time, then closed it. Whatever she might document later—whatever contradictions or complications might emerge—would have to be recorded carefully. The system expected consistency. It expected coherence. And her role, as she understood it, was to ensure that what entered the official record could be defended, cited, and replicated.

Even if the truth was something else entirely.

The red light remained steady, patient, recording everything that mattered and nothing that didn't.

CHAPTER 2
TRAINING

TRAINING DID NOT BEGIN with danger.

It began with routine.

The days were numbered and color-coded, their sequence engineered to feel earned rather than imposed. Physical conditioning in the mornings —rowing machines that simulated the resistance they'd never feel in transit, resistance bands calibrated for muscle groups that would atrophy without intervention, the particular ache of bodies being confused by artificial gravity preparation. Sweat dried quickly in the climate-controlled air, moisture wicked away by ventilation systems that processed everything efficiently and returned nothing. Systems refresh after lunch, eyes burning from screen glare, posture slowly degrading as the hours accumulated. Simulation blocks that grew longer as the weeks passed, as if endurance could be stretched like muscle, as if repetition alone could prepare them for what repetition could never predict.

The facility sat far enough from anything resembling a town that the horizon felt instructional—flat, clean, empty. A place where nothing intruded unless invited, where the world outside could be forgotten in favor of the world they were building together.

They wore identical flight-gray during daylight hours, the uniformity designed to reinforce cohesion, to make them indistinguishable from one another in group photographs and training footage. At night, the uniforms softened into personal clothing, but habits lingered. Hale still rose first, already dressed and composed when the lights shifted from night-cycle blue to morning white. Rourke dismantled irritations—

fitness equipment with a squeak, a galley latch that resisted closure—then reassembled them with unnecessary precision, the kind of attention that suggested he was solving problems no one else had noticed. Chen stayed late in the lab, chasing edge cases no one had asked him to solve, running simulations that tested scenarios beyond the mission parameters as if preparing for failures the framework hadn't imagined. Okoye rewrote notes she already knew by heart, the motion of the pen steadying her hands in a way that typing never could, each word traced deliberately as if permanence required physical contact. Jonah moved between systems like a custodian of invisible load, fixing things quietly, never announcing repairs, simply ensuring that small failures never accumulated into larger ones.

Mara noticed that.

She noticed everything, in fact—it was her job to notice. But Jonah's quiet competence felt different, less like duty and more like instinct. He anticipated needs before they were voiced, appeared at stress points before they became crises. It was the kind of presence that made a crew function smoothly while remaining almost invisible in the record, and Mara wondered sometimes how she was supposed to document something that worked precisely because it didn't draw attention to itself.

The first isolation simulation lasted forty-eight hours.

No outside comms except emergency channels. No news feeds, no weather updates, no casual contact with the world beyond the facility's perimeter. The simulation reduced their universe to the six of them and the low, constant hum of machinery doing exactly what it was designed to do—life support cycling air, water recyclers processing waste, power systems maintaining the baseline that kept everything else operational.

"Baseline check," Mara said, seated at the table that pretended to be communal, though it had been designed with the same clinical precision as everything else in the habitat. "This isn't an evaluation. Just listening."

Rourke talked about airflow first, about how the habitat recycled breath until it felt borrowed, second-hand in a way he couldn't quite articulate.

"Nothing wrong with it," he clarified. "Just noticeable. Like wearing someone else's jacket."

"It's not 'borrowed,'" Chen said without looking up from his tablet, where he was monitoring atmospheric composition in real-time. "It's recirculated. Those are different."

Rourke shrugged, unbothered by the correction. "I didn't say it was wrong."

Okoye watched Jonah while the others spoke, observed the way he listened with his whole body—head tilted slightly, hands loose in his lap, attention distributed evenly across the conversation without favoring any particular speaker. When it was his turn to contribute, he said only, "Everything's fine."

Mara marked something on her tablet.

Not *fine*, she noted privately. *Operational*. There was a difference, and Jonah's choice of words suggested he understood it too—that he was reporting function rather than feeling, maintaining the distinction between what worked and what mattered.

By the end of the first day, patterns began to surface. Hale deferred in small ways—letting Chen run a technical briefing, allowing Okoye to adjust medical schedules—signaling trust without relinquishing authority. It was a performance, Mara recognized, but a skilled one. Leadership through delegation. It played well in the evaluations. It always did.

That night, during a routine systems walk-through, a simulated alert chimed and immediately cleared itself—a false positive designed to test their response protocols.

Rourke looked up from the console, hands still hovering over the interface. "That was it?"

Chen frowned at the display, already analyzing the data stream. "False positive. Timing jitter in the sensor array."

Rourke waited a beat, then deadpanned: "I was ready to die."

For a moment—just one—Okoye smiled, the expression arriving quickly and departing just as fast, as if she'd surprised herself with the response. Hale did not comment, though his posture suggested he'd registered the moment and filed it away. Mara's camera was pointed elsewhere, focused on a console display that showed nothing particularly relevant, and she wondered later if she'd missed recording something genuine or if genuine moments were precisely what the cameras weren't supposed to capture.

Later that night, during a post-dinner systems review, Chen asked a question he hadn't planned to ask.

"In contingency scenarios," he said carefully, measuring each word, "authority consolidation—how does that actually work? I mean, procedurally."

Hale smiled, the expression arriving so smoothly it felt rehearsed, already redirecting before Chen could complete the thought. "Let's stay focused on what we can control. We'll cross those bridges if we come to them."

The subject changed. Smoothly. Efficiently. The way it always did when questions approached territory that had already been decided at levels above their clearance.

They cooked together that night—freeze-dried meals reconstituted into something that approximated food, though the steam that fogged the galley carried no real aroma, just the scent of processed ingredients becoming edible through chemical addition of water.

"This is better than I expected," Rourke said, poking at something that might have been pasta.

"That's because expectations are part of morale," Mara replied, not looking up from her own tray.

Hale smiled. "She's not wrong."

Okoye ate little, pushing the food around her tray more than consuming it. No one commented, though Mara logged it: *Crew member two: reduced appetite, day one. Monitor.*

The second simulation lasted ten days.

Sleep schedules desynchronized deliberately, lighting adjusted to mimic the long transit conditions they'd experience en route to Mars. Time softened at the edges, days blurring into shifts, shifts blurring into cycles. Conversations repeated themselves with slight variations, like rehearsals without an opening night, the same concerns surfacing again and again as if novelty itself had been exhausted.

That was when the jokes stopped landing.

On day four, Rourke questioned one of Chen's calculations—casually, the way he'd done a dozen times before during training, the engineer's instinct to double-check load factors and thrust vectors.

Chen's response came too fast, too sharp, the fatigue evident in the edge of his voice. "It's correct. Do you need me to explain basic calculus?"

The room went still. Not shocked-still—they were too professional for that. Careful-still. The kind of silence that suggested everyone was suddenly aware of the conversation's trajectory and actively choosing not to escalate.

Hale intervened immediately, redirecting to the next agenda item with the practiced ease of someone who had mediated crew conflicts many times before. "Let's move on to the thermal management review."

Chen apologized later, privately, to Rourke. It was appropriate. Professional. The kind of interaction that suggested good crew dynamics, resilience, adaptability. Hale noted it in his daily log with satisfaction.

But later, Mara found him in the galley at 0300 ship time, staring at a tablet he wasn't reading, the screen's glow illuminating a face that looked older in the blue-tinted darkness.

"Can't sleep?" she asked, though the answer was obvious.

"Just reviewing." He smiled—the commander's smile, automatic and unconvincing, the performance continuing even when there was no one to perform for except himself.

She poured herself water she didn't want and waited, giving him the space to speak or not speak, understanding that sometimes silence was the only honest response available.

"Chen's apology was appropriate," Hale said after a moment, as if he were documenting the incident for a review board that wasn't present. "Good crew dynamics. Resilient. Adaptive."

"Yes," Mara said.

After she left, he remained there another twenty minutes, tablet dark, rehearsing the confidence he'd need tomorrow. She knew this because she checked the galley surveillance later, not for any official reason, but because she was learning that the gaps between official records and actual events were where the truth lived—unrecorded, undocumented, unfiled.

By day nine, sleep deprivation was no longer hypothetical. Hale's practiced calm had calcified into something harder, more brittle. Rourke stopped making jokes, conserving energy for the systems that required his attention. Chen triple-checked calculations he'd already verified, the mathematician's paranoia amplified by exhaustion. Okoye moved carefully through the habitat, as if sudden motion might break something—the equipment, the routine, or possibly herself.

Only Jonah seemed unchanged.

Mara watched him steady the others with small gestures—a hand on Chen's shoulder after a particularly long shift, an extra coffee ration left anonymously by Rourke's station, quiet competence that distributed itself like ballast, always appearing where the weight was needed most.

She logged it as: *Crew member six demonstrates consistent psychological resilience under extended isolation conditions.*

What she thought was: *He's holding them together, and they don't even see it.*

Between simulations, they trained for Mars operations.

The Descent/Ascent Vehicle sat in the adjacent hangar—angular, minimal, built for purpose rather than comfort. DAV-1. Five seats arranged in a tight circle. Margins calculated to the kilogram. No medical capability beyond a basic emergency kit—trauma supplies, painkillers, nothing that could sustain long-term care. Fuel enough for one ascent window, with eight percent margin for course corrections. If the burn didn't work the first time, there would be no second attempt.

"Who stays in orbit?" Rourke asked during the first walk-through, running his hand along the DAV's exterior hull, feeling for imperfections that weren't there.

"Rotational assignment," the trainer said, her voice carrying the flat certainty of someone who had answered this question many times before. "Determined by crew capability assessment at Mars arrival."

"Medical capacity?" Okoye asked, though her tone suggested she already knew the answer.

"Orbital only. CONCORDIA maintains full medical capability. The DAV does not."

Okoye nodded slowly, her expression unreadable.

They practiced descent sequences in shifts—five crew strapped into the DAV simulator, restraints tight across shoulders and hips, atmosphere thin with recycled breath and the particular tension of knowing that in the real version, there would be no abort option. One crew member remained in the CONCORDIA mock-up, running orbital watch protocols, monitoring telemetry, maintaining the communication link that would be their only connection to support.

Jonah ran orbital watch more than anyone else.

He never complained. Never requested rotation. Never pointed out the inequity.

During one simulation, the DAV experienced a thruster malfunction during the terminal descent phase—asymmetric burn that would, in reality, send them tumbling into the Martian surface at terminal velocity.

Chen's voice came through the comm, steady but strained. "CON-CORDIA, we're showing asymmetric burn on thruster cluster three."

Jonah's response was immediate, his hands already moving across the orbital interface. "Copy, DAV-1. Stand by for corrective parameters."

Numbers flowed—thrust vectors recalculated, compensatory burns programmed, the mathematics of survival processed in seconds. The correction transmitted.

"Received," Chen said. "Executing."

The descent stabilized. The simulation registered a successful landing.

After the debrief, Mara pulled Jonah aside in the corridor, away from the others.

"You're good at that," she said.

"At what?"

"Being alone."

He smiled, but the expression didn't reach his eyes, stopping some-where around his mouth where it became a polite mask. "It's just procedure."

"No," Mara said quietly. "It isn't."

But he'd already turned away, moving toward the next scheduled task, the next system that needed attention.

During the formal debrief, the facilitator—human this time, though no warmer than the automated systems—asked about stress levels and psychological tolerance.

"Within parameters," Hale said, the answer arriving automatically.

"Manageable," Rourke confirmed.

"Expected," Chen added.

Mara looked at Okoye. Okoye met her gaze for half a second, then looked away, and in that fractional moment Mara saw something—

doubt, maybe, or recognition that the framework they were operating within had edges they hadn't fully explored yet.

"Fine," Jonah said.

Between simulations, there were ethics modules—decision trees projected onto clean white walls, hypotheticals presented in neutral tones, scenarios that always resolved cleanly because the variables had been carefully controlled.

During one session, the facilitator introduced a scenario: medical crisis during transit, resource scarcity, degraded crew capacity, mission continuation requirements.

"The framework exists for this," the facilitator said, pulling up a familiar document structure on the projection screen. "Modified Care Protocol allows mission preservation while maintaining crew viability within sustainable parameters."

Chen raised his hand, the gesture tentative. "In that scenario, would surface operations continue?"

"Surface operations would proceed with available crew," the facilitator said without hesitation. "Orbital watch would be maintained by crew members whose capability assessment supports mission-critical functions."

The tone hadn't changed. The screen advanced to the next slide before Chen could formulate a follow-up question.

The scenario resolved the way it always did—with better data arriving, someone's condition improving, the crisis dissolving into manageable parameters. Someone always got better in the simulations. The numbers always came back into acceptable ranges.

Chen looked at his hands, studying them as if they belonged to someone else. He'd trained as a physician before switching to engineering, had spent two years in emergency medicine before deciding he preferred systems that behaved predictably. He knew what medical dissolution looked like—the way a body failed in stages, the cascade of complications that no intervention could reverse.

This wasn't it.

This was math that assumed recovery because the alternative couldn't be modeled cleanly.

On the final day of training, they were commended in a brief ceremony that felt more like a systems check than a celebration.

Exceptional cohesion.

Above-average stress tolerance.

Clear leadership dynamics.

A photograph was taken for the official record. In it, they all smiled—professional expressions that would reproduce well in press releases and mission documentation. Hale's hand rested on Jonah's shoulder, the gesture unconscious, almost paternal. Jonah stood very still, maintaining the expression required of him.

Mara looked at the photograph later and thought: *This is the version that will be remembered. Not what we are, but what we looked like when we were told to look ready.*

As they left the facility, the horizon opened again—real sky, real distance, the world beyond the controlled environment suddenly vast and unstructured.

Hale paused at the exit, just briefly, as if orienting himself to gravity and space he hadn't felt in weeks. "Good work," he said, the words encompassing all of them.

They nodded. Smiled. Dispersed into cars bound for separate cities, ten days of personal time before launch, before the training became real and the simulations became consequences.

That night, in his sister's apartment three time zones away, Jonah called home. The connection lagged just enough to make the voices feel distant, already archived, as if the conversation were being recorded for future playback rather than happening in real time.

He told his sister everything was going well.

He told her he was ready.

Both were true.

What they were ready to become—what the training had prepared them for and what it had left unaddressed—that was still ahead, waiting in the mathematics they hadn't questioned and the scenarios they'd resolved too cleanly.

CHAPTER 3

ONSET

ABOARD *CONCORDIA*, the symptom did not announce itself.

It arrived as inconvenience.

A mild fever, the kind that might resolve with rest and hydration. A stiffness in the joints that resisted stretching but didn't prevent movement. Nothing that rose to the level of alarm, nothing that demanded immediate intervention. The onboard medical systems flagged it the way they flagged hundreds of minor deviations every day—color-coded, contextualized, nested inside probability matrices that assumed resolution because most problems resolved themselves given time. The alert appeared briefly on Okoye's monitoring screen, then collapsed into a secondary menu where it waited without urgency, one data point among thousands.

Jonah Reyes mentioned it in passing while securing a storage panel in the hab module, his voice casual, almost apologetic.

"Feel a little off," he said. Not complaint—Jonah didn't complain. Inventory. A status report delivered to no one in particular.

Okoye looked up from her tablet, where she'd been reviewing the crew's aggregate health metrics, all of which had been trending within expected parameters until now. "How long?"

"Couple hours. Maybe more. Hard to tell." He continued working as he spoke, fingers moving through the familiar sequence of checking panel seals, his efficiency unchanged.

She scanned him visually before approaching, the physician's practiced assessment that preceded instrumentation. Skin warm to the touch but not hot—low-grade fever, nothing alarming. Pupils responsive to the habitat's lighting. Gait unchanged as he moved between stations. He still moved the same way he always did—economical, anticipatory, already adjusting his body's center of mass to compensate for the panel's weight before it shifted in his hands.

"Hydrate," she said, making the recommendation casual rather than clinical. "Come see me after shift and we'll run a panel."

He nodded and returned to his work, fingers already moving to the next task in the sequence he'd internalized months ago.

Mara watched from across the habitat, seated at her workstation with multiple screens displaying logs and telemetry data. She noticed a hesitation at the ladder when Jonah moved to the upper level—a fractional pause before committing his weight, a momentary calculation that hadn't been there before. The delay was just long enough to register in her awareness, too small to justify interruption or comment, but present nonetheless.

She logged it anyway.

Crew member six reports malaise. Physical performance nominal but subjective complaint noted. Monitor for progression.

The mission plan was unforgiving in its precision: eighteen months outbound transit, three weeks surface operations, eighteen months return. They were four months into the journey, deep enough into the mission that abort was no longer a meaningful option. Far enough from Earth for communication delay to matter, for rescue to be impossible, for every decision to carry the weight of isolation. Close enough to launch that hope remained irrationally intact, that the training still felt recent, that Earth hadn't yet become purely theoretical.

By the next sleep cycle, the stiffness had worsened. Jonah's fever climbed —slow but steady, the way numbers did when no physiological mechanism was forcing them to behave, when the body's regulatory systems were losing ground to something they couldn't identify. The medical bay smelled faintly of antiseptic and recycled air, a combination that was familiar from training simulations and falsely reassuring, like a room that had seen many problems and expected this one to be ordinary, manageable, routine.

Okoye ran diagnostics twice, watching the results populate on her screen. Then again, slower, expanding the parameter set because the initial results didn't make sense.

"Pain?" she asked, keeping her voice neutral.

"Manageable," Jonah said.

That word again. The one he always used. Okoye had noticed during training that Jonah defaulted to "manageable" the way other people defaulted to "fine"—a word that ended conversations rather than continuing them.

"Where," she said. Not a question. A demand for specificity.

"Everywhere that bends." He shifted on the examination cot, the movement careful, controlled.

She pressed gently along his spine, palpating for inflammation, for structural issues, for anything that might explain the symptom constellation. He winced before he could stop himself, the response involuntary despite his obvious attempt to suppress it.

"Sorry," he said automatically.

"For what?" she asked, genuinely confused by the apology.

He didn't answer. Couldn't answer, maybe, because the apology was reflexive rather than rational, the product of a lifetime of minimizing his own needs.

The initial blood work returned inconclusive—a result that was worse than negative because it meant the testing hadn't found what it was looking for. Inflammation markers elevated, but not decisively, not in patterns that suggested specific pathologies. Viral load undetectable across the standard panels. Bacterial indicators ambiguous, present but not rising, not behaving like an active infection. Neural response latency had increased—signals were reaching muscle groups intact but delayed, as if the pathways themselves were inflamed rather than the commands being disrupted at the source.

Okoye stared at the results, feeling a chill that had nothing to do with the habitat's temperature regulation.

These were patterns that should not coexist. Markers that contradicted one another in ways that violated the clean diagnostic trees she'd memorized in medical school. A pathology—if that was what it was—behaving as if it had been shaped to evade classification rather than simply survive and replicate.

In Lagos, years ago, she had learned that some illnesses didn't follow the established rules because the rules had been written for different conditions, different populations, different resource environments. You adapted. You did what the situation required with what you had available. You saved who you could and documented who you couldn't and learned to live with the difference.

She pushed the thought away. This was different. Jonah would recover—the body was resilient, immune systems were powerful, most illnesses resolved with supportive care and time. The cause would declare itself once the testing caught up to the presentation. The margin would hold because they had built margin into every aspect of the mission architecture.

All of these felt like lies, but she didn't yet know which ones.

She opened a comm channel to Hale.

"We have a developing case," she said, choosing words that conveyed concern without triggering emergency protocols. "Non-specific onset. Progressive symptoms."

"How concerned should I be?" Hale asked. His voice was level, professional, the commander gathering information before deciding how to respond.

"Not emergent," she said, selecting each word with the care of someone who understood that her phrasing would be logged, reviewed, potentially cited. "But trending. I'll know more after the next round of tests."

"Isolation?"

"Not yet. Symptoms don't suggest contagion."

A pause—not hesitation, she recognized. Calculation. Hale processing variables, assessing risk distributions, determining how much attention this warranted.

"Keep me informed," he said. "Every six hours until we have clarity."

By the following sleep cycle, Jonah's fever had spiked to thirty-nine degrees Celsius. His hands shook when he tried to drink from the water bulb, the tremor slight but undeniable, the kind of motor control degradation that suggested neurological involvement.

"Okay," he said quietly, staring at his trembling fingers. "That's new."

Okoye guided him onto the medical cot, her movements gentle but efficient. The restraint straps lay unused at the sides, folded neatly where they always were, standard equipment that every medical bay carried but that she had never needed to use. She did not look at them. Did not imagine scenarios where they might become necessary.

She expanded the test parameters, broadening the diagnostic net to include rare pathogens, autoimmune markers, environmental toxins, neurological indicators that weren't part of the standard screening protocols.

The system responded immediately with an alert that appeared in red text overlaid on her medical interface.

MEDICAL RESOURCE ALLOCATION EXCEEDS OPTIMAL MISSION PARAMETERS.

ADJUST CARE PROTOCOL TO MAINTAIN MISSION VIABILITY.

ACKNOWLEDGE COMPLIANCE: Y / N

The cursor blinked, waiting for her input.

She closed the alert without responding. The system would log her non-compliance, flag it for review, but it couldn't force her to acknowledge. Not yet.

It would return. The alerts always did.

Hale convened a briefing in the command module, the crew gathering in the circular configuration they used for discussions that required everyone's input. Jonah was absent for the first time since launch, and his empty seat pulled focus like a missing tooth—visible, irritating, impossible not to probe with attention even as everyone tried to ignore it.

"Options," Hale said, dispensing with preamble.

Okoye had prepared, organizing her thoughts during the transit from medical to command, anticipating the questions and formulating responses that balanced medical necessity against mission constraints. "Isolation to prevent potential contagion spread. Expanded diagnostics to identify the underlying pathology. Full care protocol to address symptoms and support recovery—"

"Resource impact?" Hale interrupted, cutting to the variable that mattered most from a mission planning perspective.

She felt everyone waiting, felt the weight of their attention even though no one was looking directly at her. "Significant."

"How significant?" Chen asked. He was already pulling up resource allocation models on his tablet, running calculations in real-time.

"Sustained full care will draw down medical reserves faster than mission planning projected," she said, speaking carefully, knowing that every word would be recorded and potentially reviewed. "Not immediately catastrophic—we have margin built into the inventory. But if the condition doesn't resolve quickly—"

"But cumulative," Hale finished, understanding the trajectory without needing the full explanation.

"Yes."

Rourke shifted in his seat, the engineer's discomfort with abstract probability manifesting in physical restlessness. "We have margin. That's what it's for. We built redundancy into every system specifically for situations like this."

"We *had* margin," Chen said quietly, still focused on his calculations. "Past tense. We're consuming it now."

Mara watched them circle it—the invisible boundary they had been trained to recognize during the ethics modules but never explicitly name in operational contexts. Clause Seven hovered between them, present without language, the framework that existed for exactly this scenario but that no one wanted to invoke first.

"Proceed with isolation protocols," Hale said, making the decision with the commander's authority that ended discussion. "Diagnostics at current expanded level. We reassess in twelve hours and adjust as needed."

As they dispersed, Chen lingered near the command console, waiting until the others had cleared the module before speaking.

"If this doesn't resolve—" he began.

Hale looked at him, patient but not encouraging. Waiting.

"The framework exists," Chen said, the words coming slowly, reluctantly. "Modified Care Protocol. We trained for it."

"We're nowhere near that threshold," Hale said firmly.

"I know," Chen said. "I just wanted to name it. So we're all aware it's there if we need it."

Hale nodded once, acknowledging the statement without endorsing it. "We reassess in twelve hours."

The isolation bay was smaller than the main medical area, more austere. Functional and clean, designed specifically for this scenario—a space where care could narrow by design, where resource consumption could be monitored and controlled. A place that assumed the worst while hoping for better.

Jonah did not resist when Okoye guided him inside.

"Sorry," he said, as she sealed the transparent door that would allow monitoring while preventing potential contamination.

"For what?" she asked, sharper than she intended, frustration bleeding through her professional composure.

"For changing the math."

The door sealed with a pneumatic hiss. The hum of ventilation shifted pitch, adjusting for the smaller volume, recalibrating for the reduced space it needed to serve. A smaller promise.

That night, Mara sat alone in the observation cupola—the small dome that provided the only window view in the habitat, a concession to psychological health that mission planners had deemed worth the mass penalty. She reviewed logs she already knew by heart, data she'd memorized but continued reading as if repetition might reveal something she'd missed.

Jonah's absence echoed through the habitat in ways that had nothing to do with sound. Small things went unattended—things he would have fixed quietly, proactively, before anyone else noticed. A storage locker stuck when Rourke tried to open it, the latch mechanism binding slightly. A status light flickered for three full seconds before stabilizing, a timing anomaly that should have triggered immediate investigation. The galley's water dispenser dripped at irregular intervals, wasting precious resources drop by drop.

Mara almost got up to fix them, to step into the role Jonah had occupied without being asked.

She didn't. The small failures continued, accumulating.

By the next morning cycle, Jonah's condition had worsened along the trajectory Okoye had feared. Fever higher, pushing past forty degrees despite antipyretics. Muscle rigidity spreading from the limbs to the core, his body becoming less responsive to voluntary control. Speech slowed dramatically, as if words had farther to travel before they could be heard, as if the neural pathways were degrading in real-time.

Okoye ran the expanded test suite again, watching the results populate with a sick feeling in her stomach.

The alert returned.

MEDICAL RESOURCE ALLOCATION EXCEEDS OPTIMAL MISSION PARAMETERS.

RECOMMEND CARE ADJUSTMENT.

ACKNOWLEDGE COMPLIANCE: Y / N

She dismissed it again. The non-compliance would be logged, flagged, escalated. She didn't care.

In the command alcove, Hale reviewed the overnight medical report, his expression carefully neutral. He did not rub his eyes. He did not sigh. He simply absorbed the information and processed it through whatever internal calculus commanders used to make impossible decisions.

"This trajectory," Chen said, pointing at the graphed progression on his screen. "If it continues at the current rate—"

"It won't," Rourke interrupted, the statement forceful, almost aggressive. "We'll identify the pathogen, synthesize a treatment, fix it. That's what we do."

"You can't repair a pathogen," Chen said, frustration edging into his voice. "This isn't a mechanical failure. You can't replace a component and restore function."

Rourke opened his mouth to argue, then closed it, the engineer's certainty encountering the limits of his domain expertise.

Mara spoke into the silence. "Jonah's role."

They all looked at her, waiting for elaboration.

"He distributes load," she said, articulating something she'd observed but not previously voiced. "He fills gaps before they become problems. His absence is already affecting cohesion in measurable ways. Small systems failures are accumulating. We're adapting, but adaptation costs time and attention we were allocating elsewhere."

Hale nodded, acknowledging the observation. "We adapt. We redistribute his responsibilities and continue mission operations."

They always did. Adaptation was the fundamental requirement of deep space operations.

Okoye cleared her throat, drawing attention back to the medical situation. "If this progression continues, we'll need to escalate care significantly."

"Define escalate," Hale said.

She hesitated, knowing that specificity would force the conversation into territory they were all avoiding. "Full intervention protocols. Continuous monitoring with active response. Expanded pharmaceutical support across multiple symptom categories. Aggressive diagnostics running parallel test suites."

"And the margin?" Hale asked, though his tone suggested he already knew the answer.

"It will begin to matter. Significantly."

No one spoke.

Somewhere in the habitat, a warning chime sounded—minor, easily resolved, the kind of alert that Jonah would have already addressed. No one moved to investigate. They were all looking at the same thing now, all aware of the same invisible threshold.

Not Jonah.

The line.

That afternoon, Okoye stood outside the isolation bay, tablet in hand, pretending to review data she'd already memorized. She was watching Jonah sleep through the transparent barrier, monitoring the shallow rise and fall of his chest, the way his breathing had changed—faster, more labored, his body working harder to maintain basic functions.

His skin had a faint sheen when she checked his temperature through the access port, heat sitting just under the surface, radiating from him in a way that suggested his thermal regulation was beginning to fail.

She turned to leave, to return to the medical bay and run more tests that would probably reveal nothing useful.

"Mira?"

She stopped. He had never called her that before—always "Dr. Okoye" or just "Doc," maintaining the professional distance the mission required. The intimacy of the nickname felt like a violation of protocols they'd both respected until now.

"If this doesn't—" His voice caught, words failing him in a way that had nothing to do with the neurological symptoms. "If I can't—"

"You will," she said too quickly, cutting him off before he could complete the thought, before he could voice the possibility they were all trying not to name.

He looked at her through the barrier with something like pity—not for himself, not for his situation. For her. For the impossible position she occupied.

"Okay," he said, accepting the lie because it was easier than challenging it.

She left before he could see her hands shake.

Inside the bay, Jonah opened his eyes again after she'd gone, finding her still visible through the transparent barrier, standing in the corridor with her back to him. He watched her shoulders rise and fall with breathing that looked deliberately controlled.

He smiled—small, exhausted. The smile of someone who had already accepted what came next, who had moved past denial and anger and bargaining and arrived at the quiet place beyond.

She turned away and disappeared from view.

Outside, beyond the isolation bay, beyond the medical section, beyond the habitat itself, the system continued to count. Mission elapsed time.

Resource consumption. Margin depletion. Variables accumulating in databases that would be reviewed and analyzed and cited in reports not yet written.

And for the first time since launch, the mission clock felt audible to everyone aboard—

not ticking,

but weighing.

CHAPTER 4
TRIAGE

TIME DID NOT PASS EVENLY.

It pooled.

Hours thickened around the isolation bay aboard CONCORDIA, collecting where Jonah lay in a concentration of attention and dread, while thinning everywhere else as if the rest of the habitat mattered less. The mission clock continued its disciplined progression—cycles marked with mechanical precision, logs updated automatically, systems reporting nominal status. But lived time, the time experienced by bodies and minds rather than measured by instruments, behaved differently. It pressed against them with physical weight. It waited for acknowledgment they couldn't give. It refused to move forward when asked, dragging like damaged machinery.

Okoye slept in fragments that barely qualified as rest. When she closed her eyes, Lagos returned—not as memory with narrative structure, but as sensation: oppressive heat that made thinking difficult, constant noise that prevented focus, the smell of antiseptic failing against rot, the particular exhaustion of making impossible choices with insufficient resources. She woke before the dreams could finish reconstructing what she'd spent years trying to forget, her heart racing, breath shallow, the isolation bay's ambient light confirming she was somewhere else now, facing different impossibilities.

The system did not sleep.

Medical resource allocation exceeds optimal mission parameters.

Recommend care adjustment.

Acknowledge compliance: Y / N

She dismissed it again, the third time in as many cycles. The system logged each dismissal, building a record of non-compliance that would eventually require explanation, but she didn't care. Not yet. Not while she still had the authority to ignore it.

By the second reassessment window—twenty-four hours after isolation, forty-eight hours since onset—Jonah could no longer stand without assistance. His muscles resisted him now in ways that suggested fundamental neurological damage, as if his body were learning a new and incompatible geometry, receiving commands it no longer understood how to execute. Speech arrived late to his mouth, the words forming internally but traveling through degraded pathways before emerging slurred and delayed.

"Sorry," he said, the syllables blurring together.

"For what?" Okoye asked, though she knew the answer, knew that Jonah apologized reflexively for existing, for requiring resources, for disrupting the mission's clean trajectory.

"For...slowing things down."

She turned away before the answer could show on her face, before he could see the anger and grief and helplessness she couldn't afford to express.

Mara tracked cohesion degradation in real time through metrics that should have been abstract but felt increasingly personal. It wasn't dramatic—no arguments erupted, no voices were raised, no confrontations occurred that would show up clearly in the behavioral logs. Just drift. The slow dissolution of the careful synchronization they'd built during training.

Rourke forgot to secure a panel after maintenance, leaving it partially unsealed in a way he never had before. Chen misread a timestamp on a systems check and had to correct himself, the kind of basic error he hadn't made since his first week in training. Hale issued instructions twice instead of once, his cadence unchanged but delayed, like an echo finding its way back through interference, repeating himself because he'd lost track of what he'd already said.

They adapted, the way crews always did. Responsibilities redistributed. Procedures adjusted. Gaps filled.

But adaptation cost time and attention and cognitive resources they'd been allocating elsewhere.

And time had become a countable thing, no longer the infinite background medium it had seemed during the outbound journey but a finite resource being consumed at a rate they could calculate.

At the next briefing, the air felt different. Thicker, as if the atmospheric recyclers were struggling, though all the readings showed normal oxygen levels. As if the room itself were aware of what they were about to discuss.

"Status," Hale said, dispensing with any preamble or easing into the conversation.

Okoye didn't sit. She remained standing, holding her tablet like a shield, as if the data could protect her from what it revealed. "Progressive neurological decline. No response to current interventions. All diagnostic results remain inconclusive."

"Rate of progression?" Chen asked, already pulling up the graphed trends on his own display.

"Nonlinear," she said, the technical term inadequate to describe the way Jonah's condition was deteriorating in unpredictable bursts. "Current trajectory suggests acceleration is likely."

"How long?" Rourke asked. The question was blunt, almost aggressive, the engineer demanding a specific answer that the biology couldn't provide.

She hesitated, knowing that uncertainty was an answer they didn't want to hear.

"Before irreversible damage?" Chen clarified, though everyone in the room understood what "how long" meant.

"We don't know," Okoye said. "The pathology isn't behaving in ways that fit established models. We're treating symptoms without understanding causation."

Silence settled over the command module, heavy and expectant.

Hale nodded once, the gesture containing both acknowledgment and redirection. "Options."

"Escalated care," Okoye said, reciting the possibilities she'd been reviewing obsessively for the past twelve hours. "Continuous monitoring with active response protocols. Expanded pharmaceutical support across multiple symptom categories. Aggressive diagnostics running parallel test suites. Full intervention with the understanding that we may not achieve recovery but might slow progression."

"And resource impact," Hale said. Not a question—a demand for the variable that would determine everything else.

"Unsustainable."

Rourke exhaled sharply, the sound carrying frustration and disbelief. "Define unsustainable."

"Medical reserves depleted before return window," Okoye said, forcing herself to maintain clinical precision even as she described catastrophe. "Even with aggressive rationing across all other systems. We would run out of critical pharmaceuticals, oxygen reserves for medical use, power allocation for life support equipment. Full care for Jonah would compromise our ability to sustain the rest of the crew through return transit."

"So full care jeopardizes Earth return," Hale said, making the implication explicit.

"Yes."

Chen leaned forward, elbows on the table, hands clasped in a gesture that looked almost like prayer. "What about surface operations?"

The room shifted—not physically, but everyone felt it, the conversation pivoting toward territory they'd been avoiding.

"What do you mean?" Mara asked, though her tone suggested she already knew.

"The DAV," Chen said carefully, selecting each word with visible deliberation. "Five crew capacity. No medical bay—just basic emergency supplies. Limited life support. If Jonah's condition continues to deteriorate, if he's unstable—"

"He can't descend," Rourke finished, the conclusion inevitable once the premises were stated.

Okoye felt the room tighten around her, the walls seeming closer than they had moments ago. "That's not the question we're answering right now."

But it was. They all knew it was.

Hale's voice went quiet, the volume dropping in a way that made everyone lean closer to hear. "If we proceed with full care—if we commit all available medical resources to Jonah's treatment without knowing if he'll recover—"

"We risk losing everyone," Chen said, completing the thought Hale had left unfinished. "We could run out of resources during return transit. All six of us die instead of just—" He stopped himself.

"And if we don't?" Mara asked. "If we don't provide full care?"

"Then we adjust," Hale said.

The word hung in the air between them, suspended in the silence that followed.

Adjust.

Such a small word. Such a vast implication.

"Modified Care Protocol," Okoye said, naming it finally, bringing the framework out of the abstract realm of training scenarios and into the immediate reality of their situation.

Mara inhaled sharply, the breath audible in the quiet command module. This was the moment training had circled for years without touching, the scenario they'd discussed in hypothetical terms with facilitators who made it sound reasonable, logical, inevitable.

Hale closed his eyes.

Held them closed longer than necessary, long enough that Okoye wondered if he was praying or simply gathering himself.

When he opened them, his face was composed again—the commander's mask firmly in place—but something in the room had already changed, some threshold crossed even before any decision was formally made.

"Under the protocol," Okoye said, voice steady by force of will rather than genuine calm, "care would be adjusted to preserve overall mission viability. Jonah would remain aboard CONCORDIA during surface operations. Orbital watch. Symptom management would be prioritized over curative intervention. Resource expenditure would be capped at sustainable levels."

"Say what it actually does," Chen interrupted, his voice tight. "Not the framework language. What it *does*."

She met his gaze, refusing to look away from the accusation she saw there. "It keeps him functional. It keeps him alive longer than nothing would. It manages pain and maintains baseline cognitive function sufficient for monitoring systems. It does not try to make him better."

Rourke stared at the table, unable or unwilling to make eye contact with anyone. "He stays in orbit while we land."

"Yes."

"Alone."

"Yes."

"And we get to go to Mars," Mara said quietly, the statement carrying no inflection, just flat observation of what they were actually choosing.

No one answered.

The silence wasn't empty. It was full of the thing they were learning to become—people who could make this choice, who could accept this framework, who could translate a human being into a resource allocation problem and solve it with mathematics.

"The framework exists for this," Chen said, and his voice sounded like an apology, like he was trying to convince himself as much as the others. "We trained for this exact scenario. The protocol was designed by people who understood these trade-offs."

"Consensus required," Hale said, invoking the formal decision structure the protocol demanded. No single person could authorize Modified Care. It required agreement from all crew members capable of contributing to the decision.

The room seemed to lean inward, the five of them pulled together by the gravity of what they were about to do.

"Jonah wouldn't want us to risk the mission," Rourke said, the words coming quickly. Too quickly. "He'd understand the math. He'd tell us to go."

"That's an assumption," Mara said, her archivist's precision demanding accuracy even in speculation. "We don't know what he'd want."

"It's convenient," Chen said, the observation cutting through Rourke's rationalization. "Assuming his consent because we need it."

Hale raised a hand, the gesture requesting silence. "Enough."

Okoye felt the pressure now—not from the system with its algorithmic insistence, but from the people around her. From the knowledge that whatever happened next would be done to Jonah, not for him. That they would be converting a person into a parameter, reducing a crew member to a constraint in an optimization problem.

"I need to speak with him," she said. "Before we decide. He's conscious and he deserves to know what we're considering."

Hale hesitated, commander and human warring visibly in his expression. "He's not—his cognitive function is compromised. Can he actually consent?"

"He's conscious," Okoye repeated firmly. "And he deserves to know."

The isolation bay was quiet except for the ventilator's low rhythm, the mechanical breathing that supplemented Jonah's increasingly inadequate respiratory function. His eyes were open when she entered, tracking her movement with effort, recognition delayed but present.

"Hey," he said. The word was effortful, emerging slowly, but present—proof that some part of him remained intact inside the failing machinery of his body.

She pulled up a chair, the lightweight frame scraping quietly against the floor. Sat. Took a breath she didn't realize she'd been holding.

"There's a decision," she said, abandoning any attempt at softening what came next. "About how much care we can continue to provide."

"When you say *we*," Jonah said, each word requiring visible concentration to produce, "you mean the mission."

"Yes."

"And when you say *decision*—" He let the sentence trail off, the completion obvious.

"Yes."

He nodded slowly, the movement taking several seconds to complete. "Do I stay aboard?"

The question was so direct it hurt—no euphemism, no protective language, just the reality stated plainly.

"Yes," she said. "Orbital watch. You'd maintain CONCORDIA's systems while the others descend to the surface."

"While *you* descend," he corrected, and she heard something in his voice —not accusation exactly, but recognition of what she was choosing.

She looked away, unable to maintain eye contact while discussing her own participation in what they were about to do to him.

"Will I—" He stopped, gathering strength or courage or both. Started again. "Will I be able to do the job?"

"The protocol will keep you functional," she said, choosing words with the same clinical precision she'd used with the others. "Stable enough to maintain systems. Monitor telemetry. Manage routine operations."

"But not stable enough to land."

"No."

He was quiet for a long time, his breathing the only sound besides the ventilator's rhythm. She could see him thinking, processing, calculating his own value against the mission's needs in the same way they'd been calculating in the command module.

"I don't want to be the reason you don't come back," he said finally.

"That's not your burden," she said, though the words felt hollow even as she spoke them.

"It is if I let it be." He looked at her carefully, eyes focusing with visible effort. "Will it hurt?"

She wanted to lie. Wanted to offer comfort even if it meant deception. But she'd learned in Lagos that false hope was crueler than truth.

"I don't know," she said. "I'll do everything I can to manage your pain, to keep you comfortable—"

"Within the protocol," he finished, understanding the limits she was operating under.

She nodded, grateful that he understood, hating that he had to.

"I trust you," he said, the statement simple and devastating. "That has to count for something."

She reached for his hand before she realized she was doing it, the gesture breaking protocol in a way that felt necessary anyway. His skin was warm, fever-heat radiating through the physical contact.

"It counts," she said, though she wasn't sure to whom she was making the promise—to him, to herself, to some abstract principle of medical ethics that she was about to violate.

Back in the command module, the system waited with infinite patience.

Acknowledge compliance: Y / N

Hale stood at the head of the table, the commander's position that carried the weight of final authority even when authority was supposedly distributed. "We need to decide."

They looked at one another—not as crew members executing assigned roles, but as witnesses to what they were about to become.

Mara spoke first, the archivist's need for accuracy making her state it plainly. "If we proceed, we name it explicitly. Jonah stays in orbit while we land on Mars. We make history—first humans on another planet. He maintains the ship. Alone. For three weeks. That's what we're agreeing to."

Chen nodded slowly, the gesture heavy. "Agreed."

Rourke swallowed, the sound audible. "Agreed."

Okoye felt Lagos rise again in her memory—not the sensory details this time, but the structural similarity. Charts. Choices. Triage decisions made with insufficient information and inadequate resources. The knowledge that doing nothing was also a decision, that inaction carried consequences just as heavy as action.

"Yes," she said.

Hale closed his eyes one more time. Opened them.

"Consensus," he said, the word making it official, converting their individual agreements into collective authorization.

The cursor blinked on Okoye's medical interface, patient and implacable.

She stepped forward.

She pressed **Y**.

The cursor stopped blinking.

Text appeared, populating the screen with automated efficiency:

Modified Care Protocol initiated.

Crew capability assessment: Crew Member Six assigned orbital watch for duration of surface operations.

Care parameters adjusted to mission-preserving thresholds.

Surface operations may proceed with five crew.

Medical resource expenditure now within sustainable parameters.

Thank you for your compliance.

Somewhere deep in CONCORDIA's systems architecture, a subsystem recalibrated. Margins that had been bleeding toward catastrophic failure stabilized. The mission trajectory line that had been curving toward abort straightened into viability.

Across the habitat, in spaces the system didn't measure, something else shifted.

Rourke did not meet anyone's eyes as he left the command module, moving quickly as if he could outpace what they'd just done.

Chen sat alone at his station, staring at calculations he had already solved, running the numbers again as if repetition might change the result or absolve him of complicity.

Hale returned to his quarters and closed the hatch—the first time he'd sought privacy since launch, the first time he'd opted out of the communal space they'd inhabited for months.

Mara stood in the corridor, listening to the habitat's ambient hum—the ventilation, the power systems, the life support that kept them all alive. It sounded the same as before.

Only it wasn't.

In the isolation bay, Jonah slept. The ventilator continued its rhythm, now supplemented by the Modified Care Protocol's automated systems —pain management on a timer, fluid regulation optimized for maintenance rather than recovery, monitoring reduced to the minimum necessary to prevent catastrophic failure.

The system had accepted their decision.

They had converted him into infrastructure.

CHAPTER 5
AFTERCARE

CONCORDIA ADJUSTED—HABITAT first, then systems, then people.

Lighting cycles shifted automatically, responding to the new resource allocation priorities. Common areas brightened by three percent, the increase subtle enough that no one consciously noticed but sufficient to boost alertness metrics. The medical bay dimmed to minimum operational levels, conserving power now that active treatment had been replaced by maintenance monitoring. Water rations increased by two percent across the crew, the marginal improvement in hydration offsetting stress-related physiological impacts. Power rerouted from diagnostic equipment that was no longer running continuous cycles. Schedules recalibrated to distribute Jonah's former responsibilities across the remaining crew.

Small things. Measurable things. Changes that could be quantified and justified and logged as optimization rather than consequence.

The margins had stabilized. They could all feel it, the way you felt a headache ease—not gone, just contained within manageable parameters. The mission trajectory that had been bleeding toward abort had straightened back into viability.

Life continued.

Okoye noticed the change first.

Not because the system flagged anything—it didn't, because everything was operating within acceptable parameters—but because the medical bay had developed a rhythm she had come to recognize despite herself.

Since Jonah's transfer to the Modified Care Protocol, the ventilator's cadence had been steady: a low, regular cycle of mechanical breathing that she no longer consciously tracked but that had become part of the bay's ambient signature.

Now there was a pause where none had been before.

Barely a pause. A hesitation between cycles, the briefest interruption in the rhythm. The numbers on the vital signs display remained within tolerance. No alerts surfaced on her medical interface. The system registered no deviation requiring intervention.

Then the rhythm resumed, smooth and even, as if nothing had happened.

Jonah did not wake.

Not fully. Not in any way that would register as consciousness in the medical sense. He drifted in a narrow band of semi-awareness—eyes opening without focus, tracking movement without recognition. Hands twitching as if remembering tasks they could no longer complete, muscle memory persisting after cognition had degraded. Fluids cycled through IV lines on automated schedules. Pain was managed precisely, economically, titrated to the minimum dosage necessary to prevent distress signals without wasting resources on comfort beyond that threshold.

The medical bay remained physically unchanged, but it had transformed functionally into something else. A closed system—entered for monitoring, exited after data collection, never inhabited. The space where care had once meant healing now meant maintenance. Preservation without recovery.

Okoye checked on him every four hours. Not because the protocol required it—it didn't, automated monitoring was sufficient for the parameters they were tracking—but because she needed to look at him directly and verify whether anything had changed.

It never had. The consistency was mathematically perfect, vitals held within the narrow bands the protocol specified.

That constancy frightened her more than decline would have. Decline would have meant progression, a trajectory that eventually resolved. This was suspension, indefinite and stable.

She spoke to him anyway, during the checks that weren't required.

"I'm here," she said.

The words were not recorded by any system. They served no medical purpose, contributed nothing to the data logs. But she said them anyway, as if saying them preserved something the protocol couldn't measure.

The medical interface no longer suggested diagnostic pathways or treatment options. There were no branching decision trees left to explore, no expandable menus offering alternative interventions. The display had simplified itself to pure maintenance: vitals rendered as numerical values, threshold indicators showing distance from alert parameters, notification settings that would fire only when a line was crossed requiring immediate action.

A status message had appeared once, twelve hours after protocol initiation:

Care stabilized within mission-preserving parameters.

The sentence appeared once, confirmed what they'd all agreed to, then never appeared again. The system didn't need to repeat itself. The state had been achieved and would be maintained.

Mara felt the shift immediately, though it took her longer to articulate what had changed. It moved through the crew like a pressure front— subtle, difficult to locate precisely, but undeniable in its effects on behavior and interaction patterns.

She experienced the ship mostly through logs and threshold violations, inferring human states from system states. The rest she observed directly but didn't always know how to interpret.

Rourke became quieter—not withdrawn in a way that would register as concerning on psychological assessments, but focused with an intensity that felt defensive. He repaired things that did not need repairing, performing maintenance on systems already within optimal tolerance ranges. He recalibrated sensors that were reporting accurately. He avoided the medical bay entirely, his movement patterns through the habitat shifting to eliminate any route that would bring him past its sealed door. When circumstance forced him near it, his eyes flicked away reflexively, as if looking directly might pull him inside or force him to acknowledge what was happening there.

Chen worked longer hours, his already considerable precision hardening into something approaching compulsion. He reran trajectory simulations he knew would not change, the calculations already verified multiple times. He was chasing something through the mathematics—absolution, perhaps, or certainty that the choice they'd made was the only one the numbers would permit. When he slept, it was in short, abrupt intervals that left no room for dreams, waking with the sudden alertness of someone avoiding something.

Hale tightened the schedule.

More check-ins. More briefings. More structured interaction that prevented unscripted conversation. His voice remained steady—the commander's practiced calm that suggested control even when control was illusory—but his eyes no longer lingered on faces during conversations. He addressed functions now, not people. Directing crew members through their roles rather than engaging with them as individuals.

It was efficient.

It worked.

It kept them moving forward without dwelling on what moving forward required.

Okoye noticed he had stopped asking her how she was doing, the informal welfare checks that had been part of his leadership routine since training. She understood why—her answer would either be a lie or a truth neither of them wanted voiced. She did not offer the information unprompted.

The ship did not allow space for grief. There was no ritual encoded in mission protocols, no sanctioned pause for processing loss. Jonah had not died. There was no body to honor, no memorial to conduct, no clear endpoint that would permit closure. The medical systems reported him as stable. He existed in a state that was neither life as they'd known it nor death as they could acknowledge.

There was nothing to mourn, officially.

And yet—

Something had ended.

Meals were eaten quickly now, the communal aspect reduced to functional necessity. Conversation narrowed to mission-critical information exchange, technical updates that required verbal confirmation. Laughter did not vanish entirely—it would occasionally surface, brief and oddly loud, startling in the quiet habitat—then disappear again as if embarrassed by itself, as if joy were inappropriate given what they'd done.

During one meal, Chen started to speak, then stopped mid-breath. His fork hovered above his tray, tines catching the overhead lighting.

"What?" Rourke asked, looking up.

Chen shook his head. "Nothing." He gestured vaguely toward a sensor panel that Jonah used to maintain. "The temperature sensor's drifting again. Outside acceptable variance."

"I'll fix it," Rourke said quickly, too quickly, the offer coming before Chen had finished describing the problem.

They finished eating in silence, food consumed without tasting, the meal completing a biological requirement without providing any social function.

Later, Mara reviewed the meal recording for behavioral analysis. Chen had not been looking at the sensor panel when he started to speak.

He had been looking at Jonah's empty seat.

She did not log this observation. Some data had no useful application, no actionable insight that would improve mission performance. Recording it would only create a permanent artifact of something everyone was trying not to see.

Cohesion metrics hovered just above the acceptable thresholds defined by mission psychology protocols. The numbers provided no reassurance. They simply confirmed that the crew was still capable of functioning, that degradation hadn't yet reached levels requiring intervention.

During a routine systems check, Rourke muttered, "We're good," verifying some status reading, and then added quieter, as if to himself, "We have to be."

No one responded. The statement hung in the air, ambiguous—could have meant the systems had to be good, could have meant the crew had to be good. Could have meant they had to be justified in what they'd chosen.

Okoye dreamed less now. When she slept, it was shallow and blank, consciousness dimming without fully extinguishing. The absence of dreams felt like a punishment deferred, like her subconscious was refusing to process what she couldn't allow herself to face while awake.

During one check—she'd lost track of which one, the four-hour intervals blurring together—Jonah stirred more than usual. His brow furrowed, mouth moving without producing sound. Okoye leaned closer, drawn by the unusual activity.

"Jonah?" she said, knowing he probably couldn't hear, couldn't respond, but asking anyway.

His eyes opened briefly. Recognition flickered across his face—weak but present, a moment of consciousness surfacing through the pharmaceutical haze the protocol maintained.

"Mira," he whispered, the nickname emerging with effort.

"Yes," she said quickly, urgently, leaning closer. "I'm here."

His gaze slid past her, unfocused, the brief clarity already fading. "Did... we—?"

The question trailed off, but she knew what he was asking. Had they made it. Had the choice been worth it. Had they proceeded.

"Yes," she said. "We're on track. Mars approach is nominal."

He exhaled—not relief exactly, but something like release. Permission to stop fighting, to accept where he was and what he'd become.

"Okay," he said.

Then he was gone again, drifting back into the narrow band of semi-consciousness the protocol allowed. Not awake, not asleep. Maintained.

Okoye sat with him longer than the protocol permitted, longer than was necessary for any medical purpose. The system did not object. It had no reason to. She wasn't consuming resources or interfering with auto-mated care processes. She was simply present.

She wanted to apologize. To explain that there had been no good choice, only choices with different costs. To say that they'd tried to find another way and the mathematics had defeated them. But apologies required witnesses capable of receiving them, and Jonah was no longer one. His consciousness, when it surfaced, was too fragmented to hold complex thoughts. And even if he could understand, what would she be apolo-gizing for? Doing what he'd accepted? Following the framework they'd all agreed to?

She stood finally. Checked his vitals again. Everything stable.

She hated that word. Hated how it transformed tragedy into achieve-ment, suffering into acceptable parameters.

Later, Mara found her stalled in the corridor outside the isolation bay, standing motionless, staring at the sealed door.

"You don't have to do this alone," Mara said quietly.

Okoye looked at her, the statement taking several seconds to process. "I already did," she said. "We all did. Alone together."

That night, Chen found Rourke in the engineering bay long past scheduled sleep hours, recalibrating a thruster control system that did not need attention, that was reporting perfect function.

"You okay?" Chen asked, the question formulaic, expecting the formulaic response.

Rourke didn't look up from the interface he was adjusting. "Fine."

"If you need to talk—"

"I don't."

The finality in his voice ended the conversation. Chen stood another moment, uncertain whether to press or retreat, then left. Neither of them mentioned the exchange again.

In her quarters, Mara made a note in her private log: *Interpersonal support mechanisms degrading. Isolation increasing despite physical proximity. Crew fragmenting along individual guilt trajectories.*

She almost flagged it for Hale's review, almost added it to the behavioral metrics that informed command decisions.

Then didn't.

What would he do with the information? Order them to feel better? Mandate emotional processing? They were functional. That was what the mission required. Everything else was noise.

Time resumed its uneven behavior, pooling in some moments and rushing through others. Days passed in discrete cycles marked by the mission clock. Data accumulated in databases that would eventually be analyzed by people who weren't here, who hadn't made this choice. The ship moved steadily along its plotted arc, indifferent to the interior weather, to the grief that had no outlet and the guilt that had no resolution.

Hale delivered a status report to Earth, the regular update transmitted through the communications array, traveling at light speed through the void toward people who would receive it nine minutes later.

"Mission parameters nominal. All systems within acceptable thresholds. Crew health stable. Mars approach on schedule."

He did not mention Jonah by name. Medical status fell under privacy protocols unless directly relevant to mission viability, and since the Modified Care Protocol had stabilized resource consumption, Jonah's condition was no longer relevant to mission assessment.

It was not evasion. It was protocol.

When the transmission ended, Hale remained seated at the communications console, hands folded, listening to the ambient hum of systems he could still control, still optimize, still manage.

Stable, he had reported.

Not recovered.

Not improving.

Not conscious in any meaningful sense.

Stable.

One cycle later, a minor alert sounded in the medical bay. Not an emergency—nothing requiring immediate response. Just a threshold crossed, a parameter reaching the edge of its acceptable range exactly as the protocol's predictive models had calculated it would.

Okoye acknowledged the alert. Pulled up the medication interface. Made the adjustment the system recommended.

She reduced the antibiotic dosage from therapeutic to prophylactic levels. No longer fighting infection, just preventing new ones. Then the anti-inflammatory, dialing it back because the inflammation had plateaued. Then the supplemental nutrition, reducing from optimal intake to minimal maintenance calories.

Each change small enough to justify individually. Each one following the protocol's guidance. Each one technically reversible, though reversal would consume resources they'd agreed not to spend.

Each one irreversible in practice.

The protocol offered these recommendations automatically, displaying them on her interface with the same neutral efficiency it displayed everything else. It was optimizing care within the constraints they'd established, making rational micro-adjustments to maintain stability at minimum cost.

She could have refused them. Could have maintained higher dosages, consumed more resources, pushed against the framework's boundaries.

She did not.

In the habitat beyond the medical bay, routines absorbed Jonah's absence. His former responsibilities had been redistributed and normalized. His name faded from daily briefings, appearing only in medical logs that most crew members didn't access. His chair at the meal table remained empty, but unremarked upon—they'd unconsciously adjusted their seating pattern to eliminate the visual gap, spacing themselves differently so the absence was less obvious.

They adapted.

They were good at adapting.

Somewhere beneath the steady hum of life support systems, beneath the metrics and margins and quiet compliance with the framework they'd agreed to, a different kind of accounting began.

One with no interface to display it.

No alerts to mark its thresholds.

No protocol to optimize it.

Only memory.

Only weight.

Outside the pressure hull, Mars grew larger in the viewports with each passing day—red, cold, inevitable. The planet that had justified everything, that had made the choice necessary, that would vindicate the sacrifice if they reached it successfully.

The mission proceeded exactly as planned.

That was the part none of them could bear to look at directly.

CHAPTER 6
RESIDUE

MEMORY DID NOT ARRIVE ALL AT ONCE.

It surfaced inside Concordia the way pressure does—incremental, localized, finding weaknesses no one had known were there until the stress revealed them. Small fractures in the architecture of who they'd believed themselves to be, spreading through invisible pathways until the structure no longer held the same shape.

Concordia remained stable. Trajectory unchanged, propulsion systems nominal, life support maintaining parameters within acceptable variance. Mars continued its patient enlargement beyond the viewports, a fact so steady and predictable it bordered on mercy—at least the planet behaved according to mathematics, at least something responded the way the models predicted it would.

Inside the pressure hull, the crew began to misremember.

Not events—those remained intact, logged with timestamps, retrievable on command from databases that preserved everything with mechanical fidelity. Not data—the numbers were immutable, verified, backed up across redundant systems. What they misremembered was themselves. Who they had been before. What they had believed they were capable of choosing. The distance between their training-era assumptions and their present reality.

Okoye caught herself mid-sentence during a routine medical systems check, about to ask Jonah to verify a calculation the way she'd done dozens of times during the outbound journey. She stopped, the words dying in her throat. Finished the task alone, running the verification protocols herself. Logged the results correctly with no indication that anything had been unusual about the process.

Later, lying in her bunk during designated sleep hours that produced no actual rest, she could not remember whether she had spoken his name aloud or only thought it. The distinction felt important in a way she couldn't articulate. Speaking his name would mean the habit was still strong, the ghost more real. Only thinking it might mean she was adapting, moving forward, forgetting.

She didn't know which possibility frightened her more.

Rourke found himself pausing before beginning repairs in the engineering bay, hands hovering uselessly above tools he'd already selected, waiting for something he couldn't name. He would stand there for seconds too long—not frozen, exactly, but suspended—tools laid out with his usual precision, procedure memorized, but unable to begin until... what? Some confirmation that no longer came. Some second opinion from someone who wasn't there anymore. When he realized what he was doing, irritation flared through him—sharp, disproportionate to the minor inefficiency.

"Idiot," he muttered once, alone in the engineering bay, and tightened a bolt with excessive force until the torque alarm chirped in protest, warning him he was exceeding specifications and risking damage.

He recalibrated and continued working, but the anger remained—at himself for the weakness, at Jonah for being absent, at the situation for being impossible, at everyone for accepting the framework that had made this necessary.

Chen began waking from sleep with calculations already running behind his eyes, phantom problems solving themselves in the hypnagogic state between unconsciousness and awareness. He would sit up in his bunk abruptly, heart racing with adrenaline, convinced he had missed something essential—some variable in the resource calculations that would invalidate the choice they'd made, some overlooked alternative that Jonah would have caught without needing to be told, without needing to run the numbers because his intuition would have flagged the error.

The thought arrived unbidden, unwanted.

He tried to replace it with certainty, with the mathematical confidence that had always steadied him. Numbers did not accuse. They only reflected. They showed what was, not what should be. The calculations that had justified the Modified Care Protocol were sound. He'd verified them himself, multiple times, from different analytical approaches. They were correct.

But reflections, he was learning, could be cruel even when accurate. Especially when accurate.

Mara noticed the shift in language first—the archivist's trained attention to how people spoke, what words they chose, what patterns emerged in communication under stress.

They had stopped saying *we*.

Instructions were issued impersonally now, passive voice replacing active agency. "This needs recalibration." "That requires review." "Maintenance should be scheduled." Subjects dropped away from sentences, as if agency itself were a liability, as if acknowledging who was making decisions might force them to confront what those decisions meant.

During one formal briefing—routine status update, nothing remarkable —Hale referred to Jonah as *the patient*.

Not by name. Not as crew member. *The patient.*

The word landed in the middle of the briefing like a physical object dropped on the table.

Then it vanished, accepted without comment, integrated into the conversation as if it had always been the appropriate designation. No one corrected him. No one asked him to use Jonah's name.

Mara logged it privately: *Linguistic distancing. Subject objectification. Commander Hale establishing semantic separation between crew and patient status.*

She wondered if Hale was aware he was doing it, or if the language had simply adjusted itself automatically, optimizing communication to minimize discomfort.

Okoye carried the weight differently than the others. It settled behind her sternum—a constant pressure that flared unpredictably, sometimes remaining dormant for hours while she worked efficiently, moving through medical protocols with practiced competence, and sometimes spiking without warning until she found herself unable to breathe properly while reviewing vitals she knew by heart, familiar numbers suddenly incomprehensible.

She began checking on Jonah more often than necessary, exceeding the protocol's recommended monitoring frequency. Then, recognizing the compulsion, she forced herself to check less, extending the intervals to prove she could.

The oscillation frightened her more than either extreme. The lack of consistency suggested she wasn't in control, that her responses were becoming unpredictable, that she was fragmenting in ways she couldn't manage.

Once, during what should have been routine vital signs review, she caught herself calculating how much longer the current protocol would sustain him—not consciously deciding to run the projection, but finding the mental calculation already complete, the timeline already projected across weeks and months. She closed the medical interface immediately, the gesture too abrupt, too urgent. Sat on the edge of the isolation bay cot—Jonah was three meters away, separated by the transparent barrier. Pressed her palms against her thighs until the physical pressure overrode the urge to continue the calculation, to know exactly how long this would last.

She did not pray. She had stopped praying years ago, in Lagos, when prayer had proven insufficient against the mathematical reality of triage. But the impulse surfaced anyway—muscle memory from a former version of herself, reaching for comfort that no longer existed.

The system continued to offer nothing beyond its initial optimization. It had done its job. The margins had stabilized. The mission was viable. It did not need to explain itself further, did not need to justify or elaborate. The framework was complete.

One cycle, during a scheduled maintenance window, the ship passed through a region of increased solar particle activity. Nothing dangerous —radiation levels remained well within shielding tolerance—but the interference created a mild communications delay. Not a blackout, just degraded signal quality that increased Earth contact latency from nine minutes to seventeen.

Without Ground Control's signal—even delayed, even attenuated—the silence inside Concordia thickened perceptibly.

Hale convened a briefing that did not need to happen, no agenda items requiring immediate discussion, no decisions pending.

"Status," he said, going around the table as if this were routine.

They gave it. Efficiently. Thoroughly. Each crew member reporting on their domain with professional precision.

When the reports concluded, no one stood to leave.

Hale looked at them—really looked, making eye contact in a way he'd been avoiding for days. Really seeing them as individuals rather than function operators.

"Any concerns?" he asked, the question broader than technical status, inviting something beyond nominal reports.

The question hung in the shared habitat, filling the space between them.

Rourke looked at his hands, studying them as if they belonged to someone else.

Chen's jaw tightened, muscles flexing visibly.

Okoye's breath caught—just enough to be audible in the quiet, a small hitch that everyone heard.

Mara opened her mouth, words forming, ready to surface.

Closed it again.

The moment passed. Whatever might have been said remained unspoken.

"Fine," Hale said finally, accepting the silence as answer. "Dismissed."

Later, Mara found herself standing outside the isolation bay without remembering the decision to go there, without consciously choosing to leave her workstation and transit through the habitat to this specific location. Her hand was resting against the sealed door, palm flat against the cool metal.

She did not request entry. Did not activate the intercom. Did not check the monitoring displays.

She listened instead—to the ventilator's mechanical rhythm audible through the door's slight acoustic leakage, to the faint hum of life support systems beneath it, to the ambient sounds that meant Jonah was still being maintained.

She imagined his hands moving through the ship during the outbound journey—anticipating needs before they announced themselves, redistributing load before imbalances became critical, fixing small things quietly before they accumulated into larger failures. Endlessly attentive. Endlessly competent. Endlessly willing to occupy the spaces no one else noticed needed filling.

The thought made her angry.

Not at him—never at him.

At the system that had absorbed his competence so completely that even his absence now functioned within mission parameters. At the framework that could convert a person into a variable and optimize around their suffering. At herself for documenting it all, for creating the archive that would preserve this as precedent.

She turned away before the feeling could crystallize into something she would have to log officially, before anger became data that required analysis and reporting.

Later, alone in her quarters during a sleep cycle she wasn't using for sleep, she pulled up her own psychological profile on her personal interface—the private monitoring logs she kept separate from official crew assessments.

Elevated cortisol markers sustained across multiple cycles. Disrupted sleep architecture with reduced REM phases. Avoidance behaviors increasing in frequency and duration.

She had been monitoring everyone else's fracture lines with professional detachment, tracking their degradation with the archivist's need for accurate documentation.

She had missed her own deterioration entirely.

Or perhaps not missed it—perhaps chosen not to see it, chosen to focus outward rather than inward because looking at her own disintegration would mean acknowledging complicity, would mean admitting that the framework had broken something in her too.

She closed the file without logging any intervention protocols.

Chen stopped asking questions during briefings.

This alarmed him more than the questions ever had. Questions meant engagement, meant his mind was still challenging assumptions and testing frameworks. Silence meant acceptance. Meant the framework had won.

He began reviewing the Modified Care Protocol documentation during his off-shift hours—not to challenge its implementation, not to find flaws in the decision they'd made, but to understand its elegance. The way it balanced loss against preservation with mathematical precision. The way it converted ethical uncertainty into operational thresholds. The way it allowed mission continuation by redefining what constituted acceptable outcomes.

Someone had designed this framework beautifully. Had anticipated exactly this scenario and created a solution that was logically sound, procedurally clear, defensible.

The realization made him physically ill.

Precision, he had always believed, was a form of care. Measuring things accurately, calculating forces correctly, predicting outcomes reliably— these were how you prevented harm, how you protected people from chaos and entropy.

The protocol proved otherwise.

You could measure suffering with perfect accuracy and still choose to sustain it. You could optimize pain management and fluid balance and consciousness suppression and call it care. Precision could be weaponized against the thing it was supposed to protect.

Rourke dreamed of his father's garage—oil-stained concrete, workbenches cluttered with components in various states of disassembly, radios humming with distant stations that faded in and out depending on atmospheric conditions. In the dreams, something always broke just out of reach. A sound he recognized but could not locate. A repair he knew how to perform but couldn't access. He would wake with his hands already moving, reaching for tools that weren't there.

One morning, securing a panel after routine maintenance, his hands stopped mid-motion.

Not from injury. Not from fatigue or distraction.

They simply did not move. Command signals sent, muscles unresponsive. Five seconds of complete disconnection. Maybe ten.

When function returned—abruptly, without transition—he finished the repair automatically, muscle memory completing what conscious direction had abandoned. Logged the maintenance as complete with no mention of the interruption.

He did not report it. Did not flag it for medical review. The moment passed, and pretending it hadn't happened was easier than acknowledging what it might mean.

Hale began exercising longer than the fitness protocols required, pushing past routine maintenance limits into actual strain. The physical discomfort provided clarity that mental processes no longer could. Pain was honest. It responded predictably to exertion. It didn't require interpretation or justification. You pushed, your body hurt, you stopped. Simple causality.

One morning, alone in the unused observation alcove—the small dome they'd all avoided since launch because prolonged exposure to the void made psychological assessments spike—he watched Mars swell against the darkness.

"We did the right thing," he said aloud, testing how the words sounded when spoken to no one.

The words did not answer. Did not confirm or deny. They simply existed, suspended in the alcove's thin air, neither true nor false until someone decided.

Okoye received an automated alert during her designated rest cycle. Not medical this time.

Psychological.

Crew affect variance increasing beyond optimal mission parameters. Recommend enhanced monitoring and possible intervention.

She closed it without reading the detailed recommendations. What would intervention look like? Mandatory counseling sessions that would be logged and analyzed? Pharmaceutical mood stabilization that would show up in her medical records? Acknowledging officially that the decision had broken something in all of them?

During a routine check—she'd lost track of which number, the four-hour intervals blurring into continuous presence—Jonah stirred. Less movement than before. More reflex than awareness. The protocol's sedation had been optimized further, reducing consciousness to the minimum necessary for autonomic function.

"Mira," he said—or something that approximated it, the syllables slurred almost beyond recognition.

She leaned close to the barrier, close enough to see his eyes moving beneath closed lids. "I'm here."

His eyes did not open. The medication prevented that now.

"Don't—" he whispered, the word emerging with visible effort.

The sentence did not complete itself. The thought, whatever it had been, dissolved back into the pharmaceutical haze before it could fully form.

She waited, hoping for more, dreading what more might be.

It did not return.

She would never know what he meant. *Don't leave? Don't let this continue? Don't forget?*

She sat with him until the schedule intervened—her own self-imposed timer indicating she'd exceeded recommended monitoring duration and needed to return to other responsibilities.

This time, she acknowledged the interruption. Stood. Left. Resumed mission operations.

Back in the shared habitat, the crew moved around the space Jonah had once occupied without consciously noticing they were avoiding it. The galley where he'd prepared extra coffee. The storage bay where he'd reorganized supplies for optimal access. The observation cupola where he'd spent off-shift hours, apparently content to float alone with his thoughts.

They were functioning. All metrics confirmed it. Task completion rates remained within acceptable parameters. Error frequencies had not significantly increased. The mission continued.

They were also fraying—the psychological equivalent of material fatigue, stress accumulating in microstructures until failure became inevitable even if you couldn't predict exactly when.

And beneath all of it, a quiet truth settled into the habitat's ambient consciousness:

What they had done was not finished.

It had simply changed form.

The guilt they'd expected to feel immediately had not arrived on schedule. Instead it was arriving slowly, incrementally, through accumulated small recognitions. Through Jonah's name disappearing from conversations. Through the way they'd learned to walk past the isolation bay without looking. Through the optimization of his suffering into sustainable parameters.

The ship carried them forward—precise and indifferent, following the trajectory calculated before any of this mattered—toward a planet that would remember nothing of their names or their justifications.

They would remember.

They would remember Jonah's hands, steady and sure, fixing things that would have failed without his attention.

They would remember the cursor blinking on Okoye's medical interface, waiting for input that would convert possibility into consequence.

They would remember the answer they gave, the **Y** that transformed ethical crisis into operational protocol.

The ship carried them forward through corridors that no longer remembered his steps, through spaces optimized for six but occupied by five plus one who existed in a category that had no name except *patient*, except *maintained*, except *acceptable parameters*.

Memory held them back.

And ahead, growing larger with each day of transit, Mars waited—indifferent to whether they arrived whole or broken, indifferent to what they'd sacrificed to reach it.

The planet would accept them either way.

CHAPTER 7
ARRIVAL

MARS DID NOT GREET THEM.

The planet turned beneath CONCORDIA, its cratered surface scrolling past the viewport with geological patience. Rust-red plains stretched toward horizons curved by planetary geometry. Dark basalt flows traced ancient volcanic violence, frozen in time for billions of years. Features they had memorized from orbital imagery during training now rendered in three dimensions—real and somehow less than real, the actual planet both more detailed and less meaningful than the abstraction they'd studied.

It did not change when they came into orbit, did not flare or darken or acknowledge the adjustment of their trajectory. It remained what it had always been: a surface of remembered violence and frozen time, indifferent to whether humans witnessed it or not.

CONCORDIA performed Mars Orbit Insertion exactly as designed.

At periapsis, 120 kilometers above the surface, the main engines fired retrograde—a carefully calculated burn that bled six kilometers per second of velocity in controlled increments. Mars' gravity reached for them, bending their hyperbolic approach trajectory into an elliptical capture orbit. The mathematics were elegant, the fuel expenditure precisely what the mission planners had allocated months ago when this was still hypothetical.

Thrusters fired in sequence, computer-controlled. Angles corrected automatically. Velocities dampened along the predicted curve. Systems reported green across the board, each subsystem confirming nominal operation. The choreography was flawless, so thoroughly rehearsed in simulation that its execution felt almost anticlimactic—no drama, no uncertainty, just machinery performing exactly as programmed.

They should have felt something.

During training they had been warned about arrival—the psychology of reaching an impossible destination after eighteen months of transit. Euphoria was expected. Disorientation was normal. The historical weight of being the first humans to orbit another planet should have pressed down on them with significance.

Instead, the dominant sensation was recognition.

Not of Mars.

Of the ship.

This was what CONCORDIA did best: move forward without regard for what it carried, following trajectories calculated before departure, executing burns programmed before anyone understood what they would cost.

"Orbit insertion complete," Hale said, his voice steady over the internal comm. "Apoapsis fifteen thousand kilometers, periapsis one-twenty. Orbital period nominal."

No one applauded.

No one spoke the congratulations that would have seemed appropriate, that mission psychologists had predicted would emerge spontaneously at this moment.

They had arrived.

All six of them.

From the observation station, Mara watched the planet fill the viewport, its rusted expanse resolving into ridges and shadowed basins as CONCORDIA's rotation brought different regions into view. She waited for awe—for the reflexive emotional lift she had imagined during pre-mission interviews, during the long years when Mars had been an abstraction she could safely want, a destination that justified everything without requiring anything specific.

What she felt instead was dissonance.

Mars was beautiful. The terminator line cutting across Valles Marineris created shadows of impossible depth. The polar ice cap gleamed white against rust-red terrain. Olympus Mons rose from the horizon with a majesty that imagery had never quite captured.

That was the problem.

It was beautiful, and it didn't change anything. Didn't make the choice they'd made more justified or less necessary. Didn't absolve them or condemn them. It simply existed, magnificent and indifferent.

Surface descent preparations began seventy-two hours later, after orbital mechanics had cycled CONCORDIA into the correct position relative to Jezero Crater, after system checks had confirmed the DAV's readiness, after everyone had run through the checklist one more time.

Jonah did not improve.

This was not a surprise. The Modified Care Protocol wasn't designed to produce improvement. But somewhere in the back of Okoye's mind, she'd harbored an irrational hope that arrival—the achievement of the mission's primary objective—might somehow reverse the trajectory, might give Jonah something to recover toward.

It hadn't.

Okoye checked on him before DAV separation protocols initiated, making one final visit to the isolation bay before leaving him alone aboard CONCORDIA for three weeks. His vitals remained stable— contained within the narrow margins the protocol allowed. He was conscious, more or less. Functional within the limited parameters that functionality now meant.

He sat at the orbital watch station, hands moving across the command console with the practiced certainty of muscle memory operating independently of higher cognition. His fingers knew where the controls were, what sequences to execute, even if his awareness of why he was executing them had become fragmented.

Orbital life support systems ran clean—atmosphere balanced, temperature regulated, waste recycling nominal.

Power margins held comfortably within projections.

He had already logged the DAV readiness packet as it arrived from the surface preparation team. Checked it once with methodical attention. Then again, as if the first review hadn't registered or hadn't been trusted.

"How are you feeling?" she asked through the bay's intercom, knowing the question was probably pointless but needing to ask anyway.

"Operational," Jonah said. The word emerged slowly, but clearly. A status report, not a emotional state.

The word landed like a diagnosis.

"You'll be alone up here," she said, stating what they both knew, what the protocol had always required. "Three weeks. We'll maintain contact, but—"

"I'll have work," he replied, interrupting before she could complete the thought. "CONCORDIA doesn't maintain itself. Systems monitoring. Course corrections. Telemetry relay."

She stood longer than necessary at the transparent barrier separating the isolation bay from the corridor, studying him, trying to memorize details in case—

In case what? She didn't complete the thought.

"You'll be watching us," she said finally. "Orbital telemetry. Surface operations feed."

"I'll be watching the ship," he corrected, and the distinction was important somehow, was the difference between observing them as people and monitoring them as system elements.

That was what the protocol had done. Converted relationships into functions.

The protocol held.

So did he.

The DAV separation checklist began that afternoon, systematic and irreversible.

The Descent/Ascent Vehicle waited in the docking bay—angular, minimal, built for a single purpose with no concession to comfort or redundancy. Five seats arranged in a tight circle. Five pressure suits already checked and rechecked. Five crew members preparing to descend while one remained behind.

Jonah stayed at the orbital watch station as the others suited up in the docking bay, as they cycled through the pre-separation checklist, as they sealed themselves into the vehicle that would carry them away.

Okoye watched him through the internal viewport as the DAV hatch sealed with pneumatic finality. He was visible on the monitor feed, sitting at his station, hands steady on controls.

He did not look back toward the docking bay. Did not watch the departure. Kept his attention on the systems he was responsible for monitoring.

"CONCORDIA, this is DAV-1," Hale said over the comm channel, his voice formal, procedural. "Pre-separation checklist complete. All systems green. Requesting clearance for undocking."

Jonah's hands moved across the controls with practiced precision, executing the sequence he'd trained for hundreds of times. His voice, when it came, was professional, controlled, empty of anything personal.

"DAV-1, you are cleared for separation. Docking clamps releasing on your mark."

"Copy. Clamps release in three, two, one, mark."

The mechanical engagement points disengaged. Cold gas thrusters fired briefly, nudging the DAV away from CONCORDIA's hull.

"Separation confirmed," Jonah reported. "Clean release. DAV trajectory nominal."

"Copy. See you in three weeks."

A pause. Brief. Just long enough to contain everything that couldn't be said.

"Godspeed," Jonah said.

The docking clamps had fully retracted. The DAV drifted free, thrusters firing in gentle pulses to establish the proper orientation for deorbit burn.

Through the viewport, Mara watched the mothership recede— CONCORDIA rotating slowly on its axis, solar panels extended like wings, the hull catching Mars-light in geometric patterns. Somewhere inside that shrinking structure, visible only as a data point on telemetry feeds, Jonah monitored systems and breathed and waited.

Hale initiated the deorbit burn. The DAV's engine fired for forty-three seconds, exactly as planned. Their periapsis dropped from 120 kilometers to 70. Mars would do the rest, gravity pulling them down into atmosphere, into the entry-descent-landing sequence that had no abort option once it began.

The descent was procedural. Mechanical. A series of precisely timed events following the choreography they'd rehearsed until it became automatic.

Mars rose to meet them—not rushing, not resisting. Simply present.

They hit atmospheric interface at 125 kilometers altitude, traveling 5.8 kilometers per second. The deceleration built gradually—one g, then two, then three as they descended into denser atmosphere. The heat shield glowed invisible beneath them, converting kinetic energy to thermal energy, ablating away in controlled fashion to protect them from temperatures that would vaporize unprotected metal.

Plasma wrapped the DAV in ionized gas. Communications cut out. They were alone with their trajectory for four minutes, trusting that the angles calculated months ago remained accurate, that the entry corridor they were threading between too-steep-burn-up and too-shallow-skip-out was precisely where the computers said it was.

The deceleration peaked at four g's, pressing them into their seats, making breathing require conscious effort. Then it began to ease as they slowed, as drag bled away velocity.

At fifteen kilometers, traveling Mach 2.1, the drogue chute deployed.

The deceleration spike was violent—a sudden grab that arrested their fall, that transformed them from ballistic projectile to controlled descent. The parachute streamed behind them, extracting momentum from thin Martian air that could offer nothing more.

At two kilometers, the heat shield jettisoned, falling away to impact somewhere in the highlands. LIDAR activated, mapping terrain in real-time, comparing what it saw against orbital imagery, identifying safe landing zones and hazards.

At eight hundred meters, the parachute cut away.

They fell free for one weightless moment.

Then the descent engines ignited—eight methane thrusters firing in concert, their thrust vectoring to hold the DAV vertical against 0.38 g of Martian gravity. The engines kicked up surface dust, creating a brownout that obscured the ground but that LIDAR cut through with millimeter precision.

Fifty meters. Thirty. Twenty.

Hale's hands rested on manual override controls he did not touch. The automation was better than he was. They'd proven this in simulation six hundred times.

Ten meters.

Five.

Contact.

Touchdown occurred within tolerance—less than two meters from the targeted landing point, within the acceptable variance for a first attempt at a location they'd only seen from orbit.

The DAV settled onto the regolith, landing legs compressing slightly, then stabilizing.

Mars held.

For a moment—only a moment—no one moved. No one spoke. They sat in their restraints, feeling the gentle tug of Martian gravity, listening to the tick of cooling metal, processing the reality that they had actually done it, had actually landed humans on another planet.

Then Hale laughed—once, involuntarily, a burst of relief or stress or something that needed release.

He stopped himself immediately, as if embarrassed by the sound.

The checklist resumed. Systems verification. Pressure checks. Power status. All nominal.

A minor alert pulsed on Okoye's medical interface display, barely noticeable among the landing telemetry.

Patient status: stable.

Modified Care Protocol active.

Orbital watch maintained.

She closed it without reading the details.

No one asked what the alert had said.

They all knew.

The DAV had five suitports built into its hull—rear-entry hatches where the pressure suits remained permanently mounted on the exterior. Each port was a circular docking collar approximately one meter in diameter, ringed with locking latches and alignment guides. The suits themselves hung on the outside like empty shells, their hard-shell backpacks integrated directly into the port mechanism.

One by one, they backed into their suits from inside the pressurized DAV.

Hale went first, positioning himself at his designated port, aligning his body with the opening. The suit's rear hatch stood open on the exterior side, waiting. He backed through the port into the suit, sliding his arms into the sleeves, his legs into the lower assembly, his head into the helmet. The backpack unit contained life support—oxygen recyclers, CO_2 scrubbers, thermal regulation, power systems—all of it remaining outside, never entering the cabin.

He sealed the rear hatch from inside, the mechanism clicking into place with mechanical certainty. Pressure equalized. Systems activated. The suit detached from the port with a twist of the release collar, and he was outside—standing on the hull-mounted platform, no longer part of the DAV's interior environment.

The others followed the same sequence. Rourke, Chen, Mara, Okoye—each backing into their suits, sealing themselves in, detaching from the ports. The Martian dust that would inevitably coat them during surface operations would never enter the DAV. The suits stayed outside. The contamination stayed outside.

It was elegant. Efficient.

It meant they would leave no trace of Mars inside their shelter.

Hale descended first from the hull platform, climbing down the external ladder with deliberate care, testing each rung before committing his weight. His boots met regolith with a muted crunch transmitted faintly through suit sensors—the sound of human contact with alien world, of achievement measured in footsteps.

"I'm on the surface," he said, the words simple, factual.

They traveled outward through multiple channels—to the DAV's recorder, to CONCORDIA in orbit where Jonah would hear them nine-tenths of a second later, to Earth where they would arrive nine minutes later already archived, already historical.

Rourke followed, then Chen, then Mara, then Okoye.

They stood together on the rust-red surface, five figures in pressure suits against the salmon-pink Martian sky.

Five figures.

Not six.

Mara raised the camera, framing the shot. The composition was perfect —four crew members visible in the foreground, Hale slightly ahead, the DAV behind them, the distant crater rim visible on the horizon.

"Say it," Rourke said quietly over the suit comm.

Hale looked at them one by one, his face visible through his helmet visor. Four faces. Four people. The crew that had made it to the surface.

"For all mankind," he said, because the protocol required it, because the mission timeline specified that these words would be spoken at this moment, because someone in planning had decided that history needed this declaration.

The phrase activated automated protocols. Flags deployed from the DAV. Signals transmitted. The moment archived in multiple redundant formats for preservation and study.

It sounded hollow, even filtered through helmet speakers.

Mara captured it cleanly anyway. Perfect documentation. She had framed the shot to show the DAV, the crew, the landscape—the composition that would be analyzed and reproduced and taught.

She had framed out the sky.

She had framed out orbit.

She had framed out Jonah.

Above them, invisible beyond 900 kilometers of altitude and atmosphere, CONCORDIA completed another orbit. Inside it, Jonah monitored systems at the orbital watch station. The ventilator maintained its rhythm in the isolation bay. Life support cycled. Power systems hummed. The protocol held him functional, maintained him operational, kept him breathing and conscious enough to perform the duties he'd been assigned.

Mars did not care.

Did not acknowledge the achievement or condemn the cost. Did not weigh their success against their sacrifice or offer judgment on the framework that had made both possible.

And for the first time since launch, the distance between where they were and what they had done could not be measured in kilometers or delta-v, could not be calculated in fuel expenditure or trajectory adjustments.

It had weight.

Memory had gravity.

And Mars—beautiful, indifferent, ancient beyond comprehension—would not absolve them of it.

They stood on the surface they'd sacrificed to reach, and the achievement felt exactly as hollow as they'd feared it would.

CHAPTER 8
SURFACE OPERATIONS

THEY NAMED the first day a success.

The designation came easily, arrived without deliberation or debate. It was written into the mission logs with Hale's commander authorization and transmitted to Earth through the relay network—CONCORDIA to ground stations to mission control, the data traveling at light speed across millions of kilometers to arrive nine minutes later already archived, already historical.

Metrics supported the designation. Anchor tension along the habitat perimeter measured within predicted tolerances. Power output from the small nuclear reactor exceeded baseline requirements by twelve percent. Atmospheric readings inside the pressurized volume confirmed stable oxygen levels, acceptable CO_2 scrubbing, humidity controlled. Surface temperature fluctuations smoothed by the regolith berms packed around the habitat's exterior.

Success was a category with defined parameters.

They had met its requirements.

Surface operations commenced on schedule, following the timeline established before launch, before any of them understood what following timelines would cost.

The language mattered. It always did. Words shaped reality, determined what could be acknowledged and what had to remain unspoken.

Mars did not resist them. It did not welcome them either. The planet absorbed their presence the way it absorbed everything—slowly, without interest, incorporating human activity into geological processes that operated on timescales that made their entire mission statistically insignificant. Their boots left impressions in the fine regolith that held their shape for seconds before softening at the edges, dust particles settling back into patterns older than intention, older than life itself.

Rourke took the lead on structural deployment operations—the physical work of securing the habitat to the Martian surface, making permanent what had been provisional. Anchors driven into regolith with pneumatic hammers, the impacts transmitted through his suit as vibrations he could feel in his bones. Seals tested along connection points between habitat sections. Pressurization confirmed at the lower deck where the habitat skirt met carefully leveled ground.

His hands did not fail him today. Did not freeze or hesitate or refuse commands the way they had aboard CONCORDIA. The work was physical, unambiguous—torque values that either met specifications or didn't, load distribution that either balanced correctly or required adjustment, problems that either resolved or persisted. Binary outcomes. Clear causality.

He preferred that. Needed it, maybe. The certainty of mechanical systems responding predictably to applied force.

Chen ran atmospheric sampling protocols with almost ceremonial care, treating each measurement as if it carried significance beyond data collection. He narrated the process for the official record, voice precise and controlled, explaining methodology and significance in the tone they'd been trained to use when creating content that would be reviewed by scientific committees and taught in future mission briefings.

The numbers were good. Better than orbital measurements had predicted, actually—atmospheric composition more stable, dust particulate counts lower than worst-case projections. The margin expanded, just slightly. Resources that had been allocated as contingency could be reassigned to extended operations.

"Favorable conditions," he said into the comm, then caught himself, correcting before *lucky* could settle into the record. Luck wasn't scientific. Luck implied chance rather than careful planning. "Atmospheric stability exceeds baseline projections by point-seven standard deviations."

Better. Quantified. Defensible.

Mara documented the procedures systematically, building the visual archive that would define how this mission was remembered. Wide shots establishing context—the habitat half-buried in its protective berms, the DAV standing on its landing legs in the middle distance, the ancient delta rising beyond the crater floor. Close-ups showing detail—a gloved hand tightening a coupling, precise and deliberate. A boot print beside a calibration marker, human scale against alien geology. The footage would be reviewed, excerpted, edited into documentary segments, taught in classrooms to students who would study this mission as precedent.

She framed every shot carefully, conscious that composition created narrative, that what she chose to include and exclude would shape interpretation.

Hale moved between the crew members, issuing directives, acknowledging task completions, maintaining the command presence that held operations together. His voice remained steady as he logged successes in real time, building the narrative that would reach Earth hours later and be received as confirmation that the mission remained on track, that the investment had been justified, that the framework had produced the intended outcome.

Later, alone in the habitat during a scheduled rest interval, reviewing his own daily report before transmission, he would notice the word *success* appeared seventeen times in the first day's surface log. He would not remember choosing it consciously, would not recall the moment when that particular word became the default descriptor. It had simply propagated through the document, colonizing every achievement category.

Okoye remained aboard CONCORDIA longer than tactically necessary before descending to join surface operations, running one final check on Jonah in the medical bay. His vitals remained unchanged from the previous check, and the one before that—contained within the narrow margins the Modified Care Protocol allowed, stable in the way that stability had come to mean suspended rather than healthy.

She reviewed the numbers anyway. Heart rate. Respiration. Blood oxygen. Neural activity reduced to minimum viable consciousness. Pain management pharmaceutical levels. All exactly where the protocol specified they should be.

Stable.

She closed the medical interface and sealed the isolation bay, the hatch clicking into place with mechanical certainty that matched nothing she felt internally.

When she finally descended to the surface, backing through her designated suitport and sealing herself into the EVA suit that remained permanently mounted on the habitat's exterior, Mars light fell differently than she had expected. Harsh, unfiltered by atmosphere thick enough to scatter wavelengths the way Earth's did. The illumination flattened depth perception, made distances ambiguous. Shadows clung close to objects, reluctant to stretch, refusing to provide the visual cues her Earth-adapted vision system expected.

She joined the others without speaking, integrating into the work flow that had already established itself in her absence.

They established the first sampling grid according to pre-planned protocols—markers placed at precise intervals, coordinates logged with centimeter accuracy using GPS augmented by local beacon triangulation. Chen explained the site selection rationale over the comm channel, tone brightening just enough to suggest enthusiasm, to convey that this work mattered beyond mere task completion. He had practiced this explanation, refined it during the outbound journey when Mars was still theoretical, when science could be pursued for its own sake without being shadowed by everything it had cost to get here.

Mara filmed the explanation, capturing Chen's gestures as he indicated geological features, his gloved hands pointing toward the delta where ancient water had once flowed.

It sounded convincing. Professional. Exactly what the record required.

At one point during the grid deployment, Rourke paused in his work, looking toward the horizon where the crater rim rose in the distance. The land climbed gently at first, then fell away into nothing as curvature took over. Distance refused to resolve properly—his brain kept trying to apply Earth-scale perspective to Martian geography, kept failing to calibrate correctly.

"Feels smaller than I thought it would," he said over the comm, the observation arriving unfiltered.

"Bigger," Chen replied without looking up from the sample container he was sealing. "Horizon's closer because of the curvature. Makes everything feel compressed. But the actual distances are—" He gestured vaguely at calculations no one could see.

They let the disagreement stand, both perceptions valid, neither requiring resolution.

Earth called during the second surface operational block, the transmission arriving through CONCORDIA's relay with noticeable delay—questions asked minutes before they were heard, responses stacking unevenly as light-speed lag accumulated across millions of kilometers.

Hale handled the contact smoothly, transitioning into his formal communication mode, the voice he used when speaking to people who would review recordings and write reports.

"Surface conditions nominal," he said, standing inside the habitat with his helmet off, speaking into the comm pickup. "Crew performance within expected parameters. All primary objectives for Sol One achieved ahead of schedule."

A pause while the transmission traveled to orbit, was rebroadcast toward Earth, was received and processed.

Static filled the gap.

Then Ground Control's voice emerged, carefully professional: "Copy that, ARES-1. Excellent work. Status update on crew medical?"

A slight hesitation before the next part: "And the patient?"

Okoye felt the word land like a physical impact, felt it propagate through the habitat even though only Hale was on the comm, even though the others were distributed across the work areas pretending not to listen.

The patient.

Not Jonah. Not crew member six. *The patient.*

"Medical status stable," Hale replied, the response emerging without hesitation, practiced and approved. "Care protocol remains active. Orbital watch maintained without deviation."

The words were true. Accurate. Complete within the parameters of what the question was actually asking.

They were also sufficient. Enough to satisfy the inquiry without providing details that would require further explanation, further documentation, further admission of what "stable" meant in this context.

Another pause, longer than transmission delay could fully explain. Someone on Earth discussing something. Deciding something. Consulting documentation or precedent or legal counsel.

"Understood," Ground Control said finally. "We have full confidence in your mission execution. Congratulations on a historic landing. Ground Control out."

No one said thank you.

No one acknowledged the congratulations.

The channel closed, leaving only static that Hale terminated with a control input.

They stood in silence for several seconds afterward, the habitat's life support hum the only sound, suits hissing softly around those still wearing them.

Then Hale said, "Let's proceed," and they did, returning to tasks that required completion regardless of how they felt about completing them.

During a scheduled rest interval, Mara uploaded the day's footage from inside the surface habitat, connecting the camera to the data management system and initiating the transfer protocol. The system accepted the files without comment, processing them through compression algorithms, tagging them with metadata, organizing them into approved format structures for transmission windows she no longer tracked manually.

A progress bar advanced smoothly across her screen, indifferent to content, measuring only data volume and transfer rate.

When the upload confirmation cleared, she disconnected the camera feed according to standard procedure.

There was a brief gap—less than a second, barely perceptible—between capture completion and archive synchronization, a moment when the system was updating indices and finalizing checksums.

She filled it.

Mara duplicated one segment locally, creating a copy that wouldn't be included in the official upload queue. She disabled auto-indexing before the system could assign metadata that would make the file discoverable through normal search protocols. The duplicate didn't announce itself, didn't register in any manifest or catalogue. It simply existed, copied cleanly to local storage, stripped of destination tags and transmission priority markers.

When the sync process resumed, the official record remained intact. No alerts fired. No discrepancy flags appeared. The system reported successful completion of all scheduled transfers.

She closed the interface and did not look back at the copied file, did not examine what she'd preserved separately from the official record.

She did not think of it as evidence—not yet, not in any formal sense.

Only as something that might be needed later, if the official record failed to remember what it had already decided to forget. If the archive that was supposed to preserve truth became instead the mechanism for erasing it.

At the end of the first sol, they gathered inside the pressurized surface habitat, the lower level where bunks and galley and common area occupied the space beneath the observation dome. Helmets removed, suits left outside in the suitports where contamination stayed external. Recycled air tasted faintly metallic. Sweat cooled too quickly against skin in the habitat's carefully regulated atmosphere.

Hale reviewed the day's metrics on a large display, highlighting achievements, noting efficiencies, building the success narrative.

"Excellent work," he said, looking at each of them in turn. "We're ahead of schedule on all primary objectives. If we maintain this pace, we'll complete the core science mission with time to spare for extended sampling."

No one corrected him.

No one pointed out what "ahead of schedule" actually meant, what it had required, who had been optimized out of the timeline to create that margin.

Chen looked at his hands, studying them as if they belonged to someone else.

Rourke studied the viewport where darkness had fallen, Mars' rapid day-night cycle already cycling them into night.

Okoye kept her face neutral, professional, offering neither agreement nor objection.

Ahead of schedule. As if time were the only currency that mattered. As if efficiency justified everything it enabled.

After the briefing concluded and the others dispersed to their assigned rest periods, Okoye excused herself and ascended to CONCORDIA through the pressurized tunnel that connected surface habitat to the DAV, then used the DAV's docking connection to access the mothership.

She went directly to the medical bay. Checked Jonah's vitals again, the action becoming ritual, becoming compulsion. No change from the previous check. No improvement, no decline. Just maintenance, sustained indefinitely within protocol parameters.

She adjusted nothing because nothing required adjustment. The automated systems were performing exactly as designed.

She stood beside the transparent barrier for several minutes anyway, watching the steady rise and fall of his chest, the mechanical regularity of breathing supplemented by ventilator support.

"We're here," she said quietly, knowing he couldn't hear, knowing the words weren't for him anyway. "We made it to the surface. First humans on Mars. Historic achievement."

She paused, breath catching.

"I don't know if that matters."

She did not know which *here* she meant—the physical location, the achievement they'd reached, the moral territory they now occupied.

Later, as the surface habitat lights dimmed to simulate Earth-normal circadian rhythm, as Mars became visible through the dome viewport as darker red against black infinity, Mara reviewed the uploaded footage on her personal display.

It was clean. Professional. Composed with careful attention to framing and narrative flow. Exactly what Earth would expect, exactly what the historical record required.

She tagged the files according to standard protocol.

PRIORITY.

HISTORICAL.

MISSION SUCCESS.

She transmitted them through the scheduled upload window, watching the progress bar advance, watching data convert to radio waves that would travel across space to reach people who would interpret them as proof that everything had worked exactly as planned.

She did not transmit the copied segment. That remained in local storage, unindexed, waiting.

Outside the habitat, Mars continued its slow rotation, indifferent to documentation, indifferent to whether humans recorded their presence or not. The planet had existed for 4.5 billion years before they arrived. It would exist for billions more after they left.

Inside the habitat, the crew prepared for sleep cycles that would produce rest without actual rest, efficiency without peace.

Surface operations would continue tomorrow. And the day after. And every day for three weeks until the return window opened.

So would the protocol, aboard CONCORDIA, maintaining Jonah in the state they'd defined as acceptable.

So would the silence about what that state actually meant, what it cost to maintain it, what it said about the framework that permitted it.

And somewhere beneath the steady hum of life support systems, beneath the quantified success and documented achievement, a second record waited—un-filed, unnoticed, preserved against a future accounting that might or might not ever come.

Already too late to change what had been done.

Perhaps still time to remember it correctly.

CHAPTER 9

MAINTENANCE

NOTHING FAILED OUTRIGHT.

That was the problem.

By Mission Day Four on the Martian surface, the Jezero habitat continued to report nominal status across all primary systems. Power generation curves held steady, the small nuclear reactor providing baseline load while solar arrays contributed variable supplement. Atmospheric cycling remained stable—oxygen generators converting CO_2 extracted from Martian atmosphere, scrubbers removing metabolic waste, humidity controlled within comfortable ranges. Thermal regulation smoothed the brutal Martian temperature swings, the long nights dropping to minus-eighty Celsius outside while interior spaces remained at twenty degrees. The structure had been engineered to endure neglect, to function with minimal intervention, to tolerate degradation within calculated margins.

It was succeeding.

They were not.

Routine arrived faster than expected, colonizing their days with repetition that dulled edges and smoothed distinctions. They accepted it without comment, without acknowledging that routine was a form of surrender, that patterns could become prisons.

Each sol settled into the same architecture—EVA rotations through the suitports in the morning, sampling traverses toward the ancient delta where water had once flowed, maintenance checks along the lower deck where machinery hummed, documentation sessions in the evenings beneath the dome viewport where Mars turned overhead. Repetition dulled the sharp edges of consciousness, gave them something external to focus on, something that didn't require examining what they'd become. Hands remembered sequences the mind preferred not to interrogate, muscle memory operating independently of moral assessment.

No one debated task order anymore. No one questioned the schedule or suggested alternatives. They simply executed, one operation after another, building efficiency through mindless compliance.

Rourke took comfort in the habitat's predictability, found solace in systems that behaved according to specifications. He woke before the alarms each morning, climbed down the central ladder to the lower level where the machinery lived, and ran diagnostics in the same sequence— life support first, checking oxygen generation and CO_2 scrubbing rates; then thermal control, verifying coolant flow and heat exchanger efficiency; then power distribution, monitoring reactor output and battery charge states.

The numbers behaved. They almost always did.

During a routine check of the secondary cooling loop—one of the buried systems routed through the regolith berm that surrounded the habitat for thermal stability—he felt it.

A faint vibration through the deck plating beneath his boots.

Subtle. Localized. The kind of sensation that existed at the threshold of perception, that could be dismissed as flow turbulence in the coolant lines or structural resonance from the habitat settling into the regolith bed. He knelt, pressed his palm flat against the composite wall panel beside the access port.

The vibration persisted. Transmitted through solid material, felt more than heard.

He pulled up the diagnostic interface on the display mounted beside the life support machinery. Flow rate steady at 2.3 liters per second. Temperature differential between inlet and outlet within expected range

—eighteen degrees, exactly where the thermal model predicted. No pressure drop indicating blockage or leak.

Within tolerance.

All parameters green.

He ran the diagnostic sequence again, this time expanding the test suite to include secondary indicators—pump motor current draw, valve position sensors, acoustic signature analysis.

The system agreed with itself. Every measurement confirmed nominal operation.

The vibration returned during the next coolant cycle, unchanged in frequency or amplitude—absorbed by the habitat's mass, dampened by the meters of regolith packed around the exterior walls. The structure redistributed the stress the way it had been designed to do, spreading localized disturbances across the entire frame until they became statistically insignificant.

Rourke stayed there longer than the diagnostic protocol required, hand pressed against the wall, feeling the vibration persist despite the system's insistence that nothing was wrong.

It was steady. Consistent. Not getting worse.

Manageable.

He recognized the word as he thought it, recognized its echo from another context, another optimization of acceptable suffering.

He sealed the access panel and logged the maintenance check as complete with no exceptions noted.

Later that sol, he recalibrated a power routing node that didn't require attention, adjusting settings that were already optimal, performing maintenance that served no technical purpose but gave him something to do with his hands. The vibration remained, shifted slightly in location, quieter now but still present if you knew where to listen.

Chen flagged a minor thermal drift during atmospheric sampling near the habitat's aft exterior—an area that spent longer in shadow as the sun tracked low across the crater floor, its shallow angle never quite reaching vertical. Nothing urgent. Nothing that exceeded safety margins. The regolith shielding smoothed most temperature fluctuations before they reached the interior pressure vessel.

"Probably thermal coupling degradation," he said, glancing at the readout without much interest. "Differential expansion. Expected over time."

Okoye felt the vibration through the lower deck later that afternoon while reviewing water reclamation metrics at a workstation near the life support bay. The sensation traveled through the floor, through her boots, subtle enough that she wasn't certain at first whether she was actually feeling it or imagining it.

"Is that related?" she asked, looking up at Rourke who was nearby, performing yet another unnecessary recalibration.

Rourke checked the diagnostic display, the same one he'd been consulting all day. "Secondary cooling loop. Within tolerance."

Chen, passing through on his way to sample storage, nodded confirmation. "Everything's nominal."

Okoye waited half a beat longer than necessary, studying Rourke's face, looking for something—doubt, concern, acknowledgment that "within tolerance" might not mean the same thing as "acceptable."

Then she moved on, returning to her own work, letting the moment pass without further inquiry.

Neither of them logged the vibration as a maintenance item. There was nothing to log. No parameter had exceeded its threshold. No alert had fired. The system reported green across every measurement.

Mara noticed the compensations in the background telemetry that evening while reviewing the day's system logs. Small adjustments propagating through apparently unrelated subsystems, the habitat's automated controls making micro-corrections to maintain stability. Power draw redistributing between the reactor's constant baseline and the solar array's variable contribution. Battery cycling patterns shifting by fractions of a percent, charging and discharging at slightly different times to balance load. The habitat's control algorithms were balancing itself quietly, without complaint, optimizing around disturbances it never formally acknowledged.

She did not record these observations in any official log.

There was no anomaly to record. Nothing had failed. Nothing had exceeded acceptable variance. The system was functioning exactly as designed—adapting, compensating, maintaining parameters within specification while absorbing degradation that would eventually, inevitably, accumulate beyond the margin's capacity to contain it.

But not yet. Not today.

Surface work continued.

They rotated through the suitports in practiced silence, each crew member backing through their assigned port into the EVA suit that remained permanently mounted on the exterior hull. The rear-entry hatches sealed behind them with mechanical certainty. The design worked exactly as intended—dust stayed outside, contamination remained external, Mars never entered their living space. Air stayed in. The boundary remained clear.

Chen led a geological traverse toward the delta, narrating sampling protocols over the comm with voice that carried just enough energy to sound purposeful, to suggest that the work mattered beyond mere task completion. He had learned that tone mattered in recordings, that how you said things shaped how they were interpreted by distant audiences who would never experience the context directly.

Rourke drove anchors for a new sensor array into regolith that resisted just enough to feel real, to provide the satisfying feedback of physical work producing measurable results. His hands remained steady throughout the operation, no freezing, no hesitation. The work was unambiguous.

Okoye ran medical checks before and after each EVA, monitoring the crew's physiological adaptation to Martian operations. Hydration levels marginal but acceptable. Sleep quality irregular but not yet problematic. Muscle fatigue expected given the workload. Radiation exposure accumulating within projected dose limits.

Everything stable.

That word again.

Mara filmed it all—the habitat half-buried beneath its protective berms like something prehistoric emerging from geology, the suitports opening like mechanical gills when crew members entered and exited, tools biting into soil untouched for billions of years. The footage looked clean, intentional, composed with professional attention to framing and narrative flow.

Historical.

Hale reviewed the daily status summary from the communications station beneath the dome viewport, the document auto-generated from sensor feeds and task completion logs.

All systems nominal.

Surface operations proceeding as planned.

No maintenance exceptions requiring attention.

No action items pending escalation.

He approved the report without modification, authorizing its transmission to Earth where it would arrive nine minutes later and be received as confirmation that everything remained on track.

By the next sol, the vibration in the secondary cooling loop had not worsened.

Mission efficiency metrics held steady.

No alert fired.

The habitat continued to function—breathing recycled air, warming frigid nights, processing water through closed-loop systems, maintaining Earth-normal pressure inside its 900 cubic meters of borrowed atmosphere.

That was the lesson emerging from daily operations, the principle that revealed itself through accumulated experience:

Maintenance, it turned out, was not the act of fixing things that had broken.

It was the practice of deciding what could be allowed to persist.

What degradation was acceptable. What vibrations could be tolerated. What deviations from ideal performance remained "within tolerance" and therefore didn't require intervention.

On Mars, persistence counted as success.

For now.

Orbit: Day Four of Surface Operations

CONCORDIA remained in orbital night longer than the mission timeline had predicted, Mars' rotation and the mothership's trajectory combining to extend shadow periods beyond the averaged calculations. The planet below reflected less light than the atmospheric models had predicted, its surface absorbing solar illumination without returning much to space—dust and iron oxides and ancient geology drinking photons and converting them to heat that radiated away in infrared wavelengths invisible to human eyes.

Jonah did not see any of it. The viewport in the isolation bay had been occluded weeks ago—intentionally, by protocol—to regulate circadian cues that no longer applied to his fragmented existence. Light and darkness cycled according to programmed schedules that had nothing to do with his actual location in space, nothing to do with what Mars was doing outside.

He drifted in shallow intervals between states that weren't quite sleep and weren't quite waking. A managed condition, consciousness reduced to the minimum necessary for basic cognitive function, held in place by pharmaceutical pumps and automated systems that balanced sedation against awareness with algorithmic precision.

When awareness surfaced, it did so without context, without the narrative continuity that normal consciousness provided.

A sound registered first—the steady hum of circulation fans moving recycled air through the isolation bay. Then tactile sensation: pressure against his back where the medical cot supported him, restraints crossing his chest and hips with gentle but firm constraint. The faint pull of artificial gravity—CONCORDIA's slow rotation creating centrifugal acceleration, familiar vectors that his body recognized even when his mind couldn't process what they meant.

He opened his eyes.

The ceiling resolved slowly, details emerging from blur. White composite panels. Recessed lighting strips dimmed to minimize stimulus. Medical equipment mounted along the walls. Not Earth-normal architecture. Not surface-normal either—no regolith weight pressing down, no sense of planetary mass beneath.

Orbital.

CONCORDIA.

For a moment—brief, disorienting—relief moved through him. A confused emotional response based on incomplete processing: they hadn't landed yet. The descent hadn't happened. There was still time for something to change, for the trajectory to alter, for the decision to be unmade.

He tried to lift his hand, to confirm motor function, to verify that his body still responded to voluntary commands.

The neural signal transmitted. Traveled down efferent pathways. Reached the motor units in his arm.

The muscles received it, considered it, declined to execute.

His hand did not move.

Not paralysis—he could feel sensation, could sense his fingers against the cot surface. But the connection between intention and action had degraded beyond reliable function. Commands went out. Nothing came back.

A voice spoke somewhere outside the isolation bay—muffled by bulkheads, distorted by distance and acoustics. He could not identify who was speaking, could not parse the words, could only register that someone else was present aboard the ship, that he was not completely alone even if he was functionally isolated.

He waited for the next thing to happen, for the awareness to either sharpen into clarity or dissolve back into the pharmaceutical haze.

Nothing did.

Time passed—seconds or minutes or hours, impossible to determine without external reference. His consciousness remained suspended in the narrow band the protocol permitted, neither fully present nor completely absent.

Later—or possibly earlier, temporal sequence increasingly meaningless in his fragmented experience—a status panel brightened at the edge of his vision. One of the medical displays mounted on the isolation bay wall, activating automatically to show some subset of the data the monitoring systems were collecting.

He could not read the specific values. Vision wasn't sharp enough, focus wouldn't hold, the numbers blurred and shifted before he could process them. But he recognized the layout, the familiar configuration of a simplified medical overlay. The kind of interface designed for patient viewing rather than detailed clinical analysis.

Locked fields. Limited information. Reassuring rather than comprehensive.

It would say *stable*, he knew. If he could see it clearly enough, if his vision would cooperate, if the medications allowed sufficient cognitive function to interpret the display.

Patient status: stable.

That's what it always said.

He thought of the surface then—not the actual Martian landscape with its geological features and scientific interest, but the operational checklist they'd trained on for months. Anchors driven into regolith. Seals tested on habitat sections. Pressurization confirmed. Sample collection initiated. All the tasks that needed completion, all the work the mission required.

He imagined it proceeding without him.

The five of them moving through the sequence, backing through suit-ports, collecting samples, documenting everything for transmission to Earth. Efficient. Capable. Uncompromised by his absence.

The thought arrived without emotional content, a simple recognition of operational reality.

It did not hurt. Didn't produce grief or resentment or even disappointment. Just factual acknowledgment that the mission was continuing, that his role had been successfully eliminated from the critical path, that the framework had optimized around his degradation.

That absence of pain frightened him more than physical suffering would have.

He should feel something—loss, abandonment, anger at being left behind. But the protocol's pharmaceutical balance had stripped away not just physical discomfort but emotional response, reducing him to pure function, pure maintenance, pure persistence within acceptable parameters.

He couldn't even mourn what he'd become.

That was the final optimization.

The awareness drifted away again, consciousness dissolving back into the managed state, the narrow band where the protocol held him suspended.

The ventilator cycled. The circulation fans hummed. The automated systems maintained their vigilance.

And in the medical bay aboard CONCORDIA, in orbital space 900 kilometers above the surface where history was being made, Jonah persisted.

Stable.

Maintained.

Alone.

CHAPTER 10
MARTIAN WINDS

THE LIGHT CHANGED FIRST.

Not suddenly. Not dramatically enough to trigger alerts or demand immediate attention. The dome viewport over the habitat's common area still framed Jezero's floor and distant rim, still provided the 180-degree view that mission planners had deemed worth the structural complexity and mass penalty. But the contrast softened. Edges blurred where they had been sharp. Shadows lost their definition, boundaries between illuminated and shaded areas becoming gradual rather than distinct, as if the planet had been rubbed gently with a thumb, details smudged into approximation.

Chen noticed it during morning atmospheric calibration, when he was checking external sensor readings against baseline values established during the first sols.

"Opacity's up," he said, more to the room than to anyone in particular, announcing an observation rather than raising a concern. "Atmospheric particulate density increasing."

Rourke glanced up from the systems panel he'd been reviewing, looking at the external camera feed displayed on the adjacent monitor. The view hadn't changed dramatically—still recognizably Mars, still showing the familiar crater floor terrain—but something had shifted in its quality. "What's the forecast model showing?"

Chen pulled up the atmospheric prediction algorithm, watching as it processed current conditions and projected forward using data from orbital observations and local measurements. The visualization resolved into gradients and vectors—a swirl of dust lifted somewhere to the south, carried north by winds that operated according to physical laws that did not care about human names or operational plans.

"Regional disturbance," he said, studying the projection with professional detachment. "Encroaching on our position. Not a global event—nothing like the planet-wide storms that can last months. But significant."

"Duration estimate?" Hale asked, already thinking about timeline implications, about which planned activities would need adjustment.

Chen hesitated, checking multiple forecast models, seeing how their predictions diverged. "Hours, minimum. Could extend to multiple sols depending on atmospheric dynamics. Hard to pin down with precision. Mars weather doesn't cooperate with detailed prediction."

Mars did not announce itself through dramatic declarations.

It accumulated. Built pressure gradually. Changed conditions through persistent incremental adjustments rather than sudden transformations.

By mid-sol, solar power generation had dropped eleven percent from baseline levels as atmospheric dust scattered and absorbed incoming radiation. The tracking motors on the solar array compensated automatically, adjusting panel angles to chase a sun that had thinned into something diffuse and untrustworthy, no longer a point source but a glow spread across sky. The nuclear reactor absorbed the power deficit without comment or complaint, its steady ten-kilowatt output smoothing the loss, maintaining habitat systems without interruption.

The habitat's automated controls adjusted before anyone needed to request changes.

Nonessential water electrolysis suspended, deferring oxygen generation that exceeded immediate consumption.

Battery recharge cycles postponed until solar output improved, drawing down stored reserves within acceptable margins.

Exterior maintenance tasks flagged in the scheduling system as *inadvis-*

able under current atmospheric conditions, moved to a contingency list pending improvement.

No alarms fired. No threshold violations occurred. The habitat was functioning exactly as designed, adapting to environmental conditions that fell well within the parameters its systems had been engineered to tolerate.

Okoye noticed the change in the habitat's internal atmosphere before any display showed quantified deviation. Not composition—pressure and oxygen percentages remained precisely nominal, held steady by active regulation. But quality. The recycled air felt drier somehow, thinner in a way that had nothing to do with measured density. As if the environmental control systems had tightened their grip, had begun operating more aggressively to maintain parameters against external pressure.

She checked the medical database for hydration guidelines, reviewing recommended water intake levels for crew members operating under various conditions.

She adjusted them downward by a small but measurable amount—five percent reduction, within her authority as medical officer, justified by the need to conserve resources during the dust event.

"Just temporarily," she said aloud as she logged the change, hearing the phrase even as she entered it into the system. Temporary adjustments had a way of becoming permanent when conditions persisted long enough that no one remembered what normal had felt like.

Mara filmed the storm's arrival almost by accident, capturing footage during a routine documentation session that happened to coincide with the opacity increase becoming visually obvious.

What the camera recorded was not motion or violence or dramatic weather—it was subtraction. The landscape outside flattened as contrast decreased. Color drained toward sameness, the subtle variations in regolith composition and rock types becoming harder to distinguish. Mars became more difficult to frame effectively, less dramatic in visual terms, less immediately legible as the alien landscape that orbital imagery had prepared them for. The footage looked older somehow, as if it had already been archived and retrieved and archived again, quality degraded through generational loss.

She tagged the clips as *environmental context documentation* and moved them to the appropriate directory structure, filing them as supplementary material rather than primary mission content.

EVA schedules shifted quietly through automated and manual adjustments.

One geological traverse toward the delta was postponed without specific rescheduling, moved to a "weather dependent" category. Another sampling expedition was shortened from planned six hours to four, the reduction justified through optimization language—visibility constraints, dust accumulation concerns on suit seals and equipment interfaces, diminishing scientific return under degraded observation conditions.

"Tomorrow," Hale said when Chen asked about the postponed traverse, his tone suggesting confidence without committing to specificity. He did not specify which tomorrow, did not set a firm date for resumption.

The suitports remained closed for most of the sol, their exterior-mounted EVA suits standing motionless beneath the protective awnings that shielded the rear-entry hatches from direct dust accumulation. The suits stood like sentinels, unmoved, gradually acquiring a thin coating of fine Martian particles that settled into joints and seams despite electrostatic repulsion systems. UV sterilization cycles continued running as programmed, automated sequences indifferent to the coating forming over the very surfaces they were meant to protect.

Rourke inspected the solar array through external camera feeds, zooming in on panel surfaces to assess dust accumulation. The particles clung where the electrostatic repulsion was weakest—at hinges where panels articulated, at panel edges where the fields couldn't maintain full strength, at the mechanical interfaces where movement required physical contact rather than field effects.

"They'll shed most of it when the winds change," he said, the statement offered to the room as reassurance, as engineering confidence in system design. "Increased wind speed will blow accumulated dust clear once the atmospheric dynamics shift."

No one contradicted him. No one suggested alternative outcomes. The statement stood unchallenged, accepted as technical assessment rather than hopeful projection.

Communications with Earth experienced subtle degradation—not failure, not even significant disruption, but a lengthening of the lag time beyond the light-speed delay that was inevitable. Fractions of a second added by atmospheric interference with radio propagation, by the need to boost signal strength to penetrate increased opacity, by error-correction protocols engaging more frequently to verify data integrity.

Not enough latency increase to disrupt operational contact, but enough to introduce hesitation into exchanges that had been flowing relatively smoothly. Earth's replies arrived feeling thinner somehow, more templated, increasingly reliant on pre-formatted summary packets rather than conversational exchange.

Hale reviewed the system-generated communication schedule—automatically optimized for signal conditions—and accepted it without revision, authorizing the protocol's recommendations without second-guessing the algorithm's decisions.

That evening, as the habitat's lighting dimmed toward sleep-cycle levels and the crew gathered in the common area for the daily briefing, a recommendation appeared on the central display.

POWER OPTIMIZATION SUGGESTION:

Suspend greenhouse module growth lighting during storm conditions.

Projected impact to plant biomass: negligible if resumed within 72 hours.

Projected power savings: 340 watts continuous.

Recommended duration: until atmospheric opacity decreases to baseline levels.

They stood around the galley table while the recommendation hovered on the screen, each of them reading it, processing implications, waiting for someone else to object first.

"It's just lettuce," Rourke said finally, his tone pragmatic, engineering-practical. Not dismissive of the plants, just acknowledging their position in the priority hierarchy. "Supplemental nutrition, not critical."

"And tomatoes," Chen added, the specificity unnecessary but somehow important to state. "Twenty-three plants total. Mixed cultivars."

Okoye said nothing. Her jaw tightened slightly but her expression remained professionally neutral.

Hale looked at each of them, confirming consensus through silence, through the absence of explicit objection. "Proceed with the recommendation," he said, authorizing the change with commander's authority.

The growth lamps in the greenhouse module powered down immediately—automated response to approved optimization. Not complete darkness—emergency illumination remained active for safety and monitoring access—but the full-spectrum lighting that had been sustaining photosynthesis shut off. Growth deferred. Development paused.

The plants did not protest. Did not signal distress in any way the monitoring systems were configured to detect. They simply stopped growing, metabolism slowing to maintenance levels, waiting for conditions to improve.

The habitat continued to function. All critical systems remained fully operational. Crew safety was not compromised. The decision was defensible, rational, properly documented.

Outside the habitat, beyond the reinforced walls and protective berms, the dust continued to thicken. Not dramatically—not enough to hide Mars completely, not enough to create the total opacity of a major storm. Only enough to mute it. To reduce clarity. To make everything slightly less distinct.

The crater rim faded from sharp geological feature to suggestion, outline still visible but details obscured. The ancient delta's edges softened until even Chen, with his trained geological eye, stopped narrating its features during observation sessions because there wasn't enough visible detail to describe with scientific precision.

Inside the habitat, routines absorbed the environmental change, incorporating reduced operations into the daily rhythm as if this had always been the plan, as if they'd intended all along to work with less.

Meals became smaller—not dramatically, not enough to qualify as rationing, just minor portion adjustments that accumulated into measurable resource savings. Showers shortened by a minute each, water conservation presented as prudent rather than necessary. Movement through the habitat became more contained, more efficient, less casual wandering, more purposeful transit. Energy conservation through behavioral modification.

No one complained. No one suggested that perhaps they were optimizing too much, too quickly, too willingly. The adjustments felt reasonable, modest, temporary.

The storm did not worsen.

That was perhaps the most unsettling aspect of it.

It did not escalate into immediate danger that would have demanded dramatic response, heroic intervention, the kind of crisis that justified extreme measures and produced clear resolution. It simply lingered, pressing gently but persistently against systems that responded by narrowing margins and calling it optimization, by accepting degraded conditions and naming them sustainable.

By the third sol of reduced visibility, the atmospheric forecast models had stabilized into productive uncertainty—probability distributions that covered all plausible outcomes without committing to any specific prediction.

"Could clear tomorrow," Chen said, reviewing the latest simulation results. "Fifty-three percent probability of opacity decrease beginning within the next twenty-four hours."

Which meant forty-seven percent probability it wouldn't. Which meant they didn't actually know, couldn't actually predict when conditions would improve, were operating in sustained ambiguity.

Or not. Maybe it would persist. Maybe this was the new baseline for this location during this season. Maybe "temporary" would extend indefinitely until temporary became permanent and no one remembered it was supposed to be different.

Hale reviewed the daily summary report before initiating his sleep cycle, reading through the system-generated status document that would be transmitted to Earth during the next scheduled communication window.

Power generation stable despite solar reduction—reactor compensating effectively.

Atmospheric conditions inside habitat nominal—all life support parameters within specification.

Surface operations adjusted to current environmental conditions—schedule modifications documented and justified.

No mission-critical impact anticipated—all primary objectives remain achievable within planned timeline.

He approved the report without modification, authorizing its transmission, adding his commander's certification that the summary accurately reflected conditions.

Later, during the designated sleep period, Mara found herself unable to achieve rest. She pulled up the external camera feed on her personal tablet, watching the dust-obscured landscape through infrared filters that cut through some of the opacity.

The storm registered in the data stream as noise—randomized particle distribution, statistically normal variation, patterns that fell within expected ranges for Martian atmospheric behavior. Unworthy of special attention. Unworthy of alarm.

Mars turned beneath it all, patient and unmoved, geological processes operating on timescales that made human concerns statistically insignificant.

The habitat continued its mechanical breathing—air cycling, heat regulating, water processing. The reactor hummed its steady baseline. The systems held, adapted, optimized.

Somewhere between one sleep cycle and the next, as sols accumulated into weeks, the crew stopped thinking of the reduced visibility as an event requiring active response.

It became a condition. A state. The way things were now.

And conditions, once accepted as normal rather than challenged as temporary, had a way of reshaping what questions felt worth asking, what standards felt reasonable to maintain, what compromises seemed justified by circumstances.

The storm persisted.

So did they.

Both adapting. Both reduced. Both calling it sustainable.

Both waiting for clarity that might never quite return to what it had been before.

CHAPTER 11

SIGNAL

THE MESSAGE ARRIVED WITHOUT URGENCY.

Not an alarm demanding immediate attention. Not a warning requiring response within specified timeframes. A routed transmission marked **PUBLIC RESPONSE PACKAGE**, delivered through administrative communication channels designed to feel optional, advisory, informational rather than directive.

Hale convened a briefing anyway, treating the optional as mandatory in the way commanders did when they understood that suggestions from certain sources carried weight that exceeded their formal classification.

Earth's communication delay had lengthened with orbital geometry—Mars and Earth continuing their independent trajectories around the sun, the distance between them increasing daily. The lag now produced small asymmetries in conversational flow, discontinuities that disrupted normal exchange rhythms. Questions arrived after the moment they were contextually relevant. Acknowledgments stacked out of temporal sequence, responses addressing queries that had already been superseded by events.

Hale managed it with practiced ease, years of training in maintaining command presence despite communication degradation.

"They're pleased," he said, summarizing the transmission's emotional content before addressing specific details. "The landing footage is already circulating through public channels. Media response has been overwhelmingly positive. Political support for the program is strengthening."

Mara opened the attached materials on her tablet, watching compressed files decompress into curated content. Stills extracted from the landing footage, carefully selected for visual impact and narrative coherence. Edited video clips showing key moments with transitions smoothed and timing optimized. Captions written in language that converted technical achievement into inspirational narrative.

FIRST HUMAN FOOTSTEPS ON MARS.

HISTORIC SUCCESS VALIDATES DECADES OF PREPARATION.

CREW DEMONSTRATES EXCEPTIONAL DECISION-MAKING UNDER PRESSURE.

Chen skimmed through the accompanying prompts, the interview questions and discussion topics that Earth wanted addressed in future communications. "They're asking about decision-making processes," he said, reading the carefully phrased inquiries. "About how the crew maintained cohesion during challenges."

"About teamwork," Hale corrected, offering the reframe before Chen could continue. "About resilience in the face of adversity."

Rourke leaned back in his seat, arms crossed, expression skeptical in a way he didn't quite voice. "They want a story," he said. Not quite accusation, not quite statement of fact. Observation.

"They want accuracy," Hale said, the response arriving too quickly, too defensively. "Information aligned with mission objectives. Context that helps people understand what we've accomplished."

Okoye folded her hands in her lap, studying them with apparent interest. She did not look at the screen where the curated materials displayed. Did not examine the suggested language. Did not participate in the discussion of how to frame their experience for distant audiences who would never understand the actual context.

"They've included suggested language," Hale continued, gesturing at another section of the transmitted package. "Sample responses. Recommended talking points. Nothing binding, obviously. Just... guidance for maintaining message consistency."

Guidance had a way of becoming precedent. Suggestions transformed into requirements through repeated application and accumulated expectation. What was optional in the first iteration became standard in the tenth.

They dispersed without formally assigning response responsibilities. The assumption was understood without needing to be articulated: when they eventually responded to Earth's prompts, they would sound unified. Consistent. As if they'd all experienced the mission the same way, as if their individual perspectives had merged into collective narrative.

Later, alone in her sleep quarters during a period designated for personal time, Mara reopened the local data directory where she maintained her own archive—the footage and logs that existed parallel to the official mission record.

She did not immediately play any of the stored media files.

Instead, she expanded the technical metadata layer, the underlying information structure that documented how files were created, processed, and transmitted. Timestamps showing when each frame was captured. Buffer interval data revealing processing sequences. Compression passes indicating how many times the data had been algorithmically optimized. She overlaid the internal capture logs—her own camera's raw recording metadata—with the public upload metadata from the files that had been transmitted to Earth.

At first, the numbers agreed perfectly. Frame counts matched. Timestamps aligned. Compression ratios fell within expected ranges for the transmission bandwidth allocation.

Then she noticed where they didn't.

A fractional truncation appeared in the timeline around what she mentally categorized as "the consent moment"—the sequence where Okoye had stood at her medical interface, cursor hovering over the Y/N prompt, the decision point where the Modified Care Protocol had been formally authorized.

Milliseconds shaved during optimization. Not much—340 milliseconds total, distributed across several compression passes. Too small to trigger data integrity alerts. Too precise in its targeting to be random algorithmic artifact. The public file that had been transmitted to Earth resolved cleanly at that moment, decisively. The pause abbreviated into something that looked like confident decision-making rather than hesitation.

She pulled up the internal logs, the raw capture data that her camera had recorded before any processing occurred.

The local copy still held the full temporal interval—the hesitation visible in the way Okoye had stood motionless, the silence that had extended beyond comfortable duration, the cursor blinking without resolution for seconds that stretched into subjective eternity before finally, inevitably, the Y was selected.

Seconds that did not alter the outcome. The same decision had been made regardless of how long it took to make it.

But the texture was different. The emotional content. The visible evidence of doubt, of difficulty, of moral weight.

Nothing critical was missing from the edited version. Nothing the system would classify as data loss or integrity compromise. The decision was still documented. The authorization was still recorded. The timeline still showed that consensus had been achieved.

But something had been removed.

Not facts. Not events. Not measurable outcomes.

Just the evidence that the decision had been hard. That it had required time. That "consensus" might be a more complicated category than the official record suggested.

Mara sat staring at the comparison for several minutes, watching the timestamps diverge and re-converge, seeing exactly where the editing had occurred and what it had accomplished.

She closed the analysis interface.

The archive—the official archive, the one that would be preserved and studied and cited and taught—was no longer a safeguard against institutional erasure of uncomfortable truths.

It was proof that erasure had already occurred. Was occurring. Would continue occurring through algorithmic optimization and editorial curation and the accumulated small decisions about what details mattered enough to preserve versus what could be streamlined away.

In the habitat's common area, visible through the open door of Mara's quarters, Hale was drafting response language aloud, testing phrasing, calibrating tone for the eventual transmission back to Earth. Chen sat nearby, offering minor corrections for technical accuracy, ensuring that scientific descriptions aligned with established terminology. Rourke listened without contributing, present but not participating.

Okoye stood near the entrance to the medical bay corridor, positioned at the boundary between common space and the section she was responsible for maintaining. Listening without participating. Witnessing without endorsing.

"The emphasis should be on unity," Hale was saying, working through the narrative framework he was constructing. "On how achieving consensus under difficult circumstances preserved mission integrity. How the crew functioned as a cohesive unit despite challenges that might have fragmented a less prepared team."

Consensus. Unity. Cohesion.

Words that described outcomes while obscuring processes. That suggested agreement while concealing the mechanisms through which agreement had been achieved.

Mara watched the language settle into place, watched Hale build the official narrative that would be transmitted, received, analyzed, archived, cited.

Outside the habitat, beyond the reinforced walls and protective berms, Mars turned without offering commentary. The planet continued its rotation, indifferent to human documentation practices, indifferent to whether the stories told about events matched the events themselves.

Inside the habitat, the signal from Earth waited to be answered—expectant, already shaping memory into something teachable, already converting experience into curriculum.

Mara created a new subdirectory in her local archive, isolating it from the synchronized file structure that automatically prepared content for transmission.

She copied the comparison analysis into it. The unedited footage. The metadata showing exactly where and how the official record had been optimized.

She did not annotate the files yet. Did not add explanatory text that would reveal her purpose, her concerns, her recognition of what was happening.

Not yet.

But she preserved the evidence. Created a record of the gap between what happened and what would be remembered. Documented the documentation's failure.

If the official archive was becoming a mechanism for constructing acceptable narratives rather than preserving actual events, then she would maintain the alternative. The uncomfortable version. The one that showed hesitation and doubt and the weight of impossible choices.

Even if no one ever saw it. Even if it never mattered.

At least it would exist.

Orbit: While They Work

CONCORDIA passed over the Jezero landing site every ninety-three minutes, the orbital period determined by altitude and Martian gravity, unchanging and predictable.

Each time the mothership's trajectory brought it within line-of-sight range of the surface habitat, the ship's automated systems adjusted without requiring human intervention. Antenna alignment motors rotated the communications array to track the surface position. Data buffers prepared to receive telemetry uploads. Communications proto-cols entered ready states, monitoring assigned frequencies for scheduled check-ins.

The routines did not require oversight. The sequences had been programmed years ago, tested exhaustively during the outbound jour-ney, refined through iteration until they functioned flawlessly.

Jonah had written part of those automation sequences. Had contributed to the orbital mechanics calculations. Had debugged the antenna pointing algorithms during simulations.

He remembered that, dimly. Not with narrative clarity or temporal context, but as fragmentary recognition. Familiar patterns in systems he'd helped create.

During one orbital pass over the landing site, sound intruded into his awareness.

Not speech. Not alarms requiring response. Mechanical vibrations transmitted through the hull structure—faint, rhythmic. Thruster corrections firing in precisely timed sequence, reaction control system compensating for perturbations too small to matter individually but significant in accumulation. Solar radiation pressure. Atmospheric drag at the very edge of Mars' upper atmosphere. Gravitational variations from the planet's non-uniform mass distribution.

The correction burns registered in his body as pressure changes before his conscious mind processed them as sound. A tightening sensation as acceleration pressed him slightly against the restraints. A release as thrust terminated and free-fall resumed.

His breathing adjusted to match the rhythm without conscious instruction, respiratory rate synchronizing with the thruster firing interval through some autonomic response his degraded nervous system still retained.

For a few seconds—maybe longer, time perception was unreliable—he was aware of motion. Not travel through space, but position relative to the planet. The sense of orbiting, of falling continuously while moving sideways fast enough that the ground curved away at the same rate.

We're still moving, he thought.

The sentence arrived fully formed in his consciousness, complete and coherent, then unraveled before he could decide whether it mattered, before he could determine what "we" meant in this context, whether he was still part of "we" or had become something separate.

A status light flickered on the far wall of the isolation bay. Diagnostic indicator. Informational only. No response required from him. The automated systems were functioning, reporting status, continuing their vigilance.

He tried to count the light pulses, the way he used to during long calibration cycles when patience was required and counting helped maintain focus. One. Two. Three. Four.

Lost track after four. The number sequence dissolved before he could establish the pattern he'd been looking for.

Somewhere below—900 kilometers straight down, through atmosphere and gravity well—the crew would be working through their operational blocks. Geological sampling. Habitat maintenance. Documentation sessions. Tasks resolving cleanly according to schedule. Metrics closing their loops, objectives being achieved, the mission proceeding exactly as planned.

He pictured them in their EVA suits, backing through the suitports into the permanently exterior-mounted pressure garments. Moving carefully across the regolith. Deliberately. Safely. The five of them functioning as the crew had been designed to function once the DAV's capacity constraints were factored in.

He was glad they had made it down to the surface.

The feeling surprised him with its completeness, with its lack of bitterness or resentment. Pure gladness, uncomplicated by the self-awareness that might have recognized how strange it was to feel grateful for your own exclusion, how thoroughly the protocol had optimized away not just physical suffering but emotional resistance.

He should feel abandoned, isolated, angry at being left behind while history happened without him.

Instead he felt relieved that they were succeeding. That the mission was working. That his absence hadn't prevented the achievement they'd all worked toward.

The pharmaceutical balance had done its work perfectly. Stripped away everything except the bare minimum necessary to maintain orbital watch duties. Including the capacity to mourn what he'd lost.

Later—or possibly earlier, temporal sequence increasingly unreliable in his fragmented experience—when CONCORDIA's rotation brought the isolation bay back into direct sunlight, warmth bled through the hull. The temperature shift was subtle, a few degrees, but registered clearly in his awareness.

Comfort. Not relief or joy or any complex emotional response. Just simple physical comfort from warmth after cold.

His eyes closed.

CONCORDIA continued its orbit, mechanical and precise, following the trajectory calculated before any of this had meaning.

The surface rotated away beneath the mothership, Jezero Crater passing out of line-of-sight as the orbital track carried CONCORDIA over Mars' limb into the night side where no sun illuminated the ancient geology below.

Jonah did not notice the transition. Awareness had already dissolved back into the managed state, consciousness submerging below the threshold where external events registered as distinct from internal states.

The ventilator cycled. The circulation fans hummed. The automated systems maintained their vigilance.

And in the isolation bay aboard CONCORDIA, suspended in the narrow band between sleep and waking that the Modified Care Protocol defined as acceptable, Jonah persisted.

Glad they had made it.

Glad to have helped, even if helping meant becoming irrelevant.

Glad in a way that would have horrified him if he'd retained the capacity for horror.

The protocol held.

So did he.

Stable.

Maintained.

Content.

CHAPTER 12
PERFORMANCE

THE CAMERA WAS MOUNTED above eye level in the habitat's common area, positioned to create the slight upward angle that conveyed openness and accessibility without diminishing authority.

Matte black. Fixed position. Active indicator glowing steady red.

No countdown. No voice prompting them to begin. No ceremony that might acknowledge the artificiality of what they were about to do.

Mara adjusted the framing with unconscious precision—rule of thirds placing subjects at optimal visual positions, eye lines aligned to create natural sight-lines, background elements arranged for pleasing symmetry. She framed out the medical wing corridor without consciously deciding to do so, the exclusion automatic, practiced. The habitat visible behind where they would sit looked clean, ordered, ready for documentation. Exactly the environment mission control wanted the public to see.

"All right," she said, settling behind the camera controls. "Whenever you're ready."

Hale nodded acknowledgment. The recording indicator remained steady, patient, waiting for content to preserve.

He took a breath that was almost imperceptible, then began.

"Hello, Earth," he said, his voice calibrated with practiced precision. Calm, measured, carrying just enough warmth to sound authentically human without crossing into informality that might undermine command authority. "We've successfully completed initial surface operations here at Jezero Crater. Touchdown occurred within all specified tolerances. All habitat systems are operating nominally. The crew is healthy and focused on achieving our scientific objectives."

Healthy.

The word traveled across the small space between them and registered different impacts.

Okoye's shoulders tightened by a fraction of a degree, a micro-expression that the camera probably wouldn't capture but that Mara saw clearly from her position. Chen did not react outwardly, maintaining the neutral professional expression he'd cultivated over years of technical presentations. He registered the word as categorical—contextual, defensible, accurate within the framing that made "the crew" mean only those physically present on the surface.

Hale continued through the opening statement they'd collectively drafted, hitting the key points in the sequence they'd agreed upon. Gratitude to mission control and the teams that had made this possible. Pride in representing humanity's first presence on another planet. Collective ownership of the achievement. Phrases carefully engineered to belong to everyone and no one at once, to inspire without promising anything specific.

Chen spoke next, transitioning smoothly when Hale gestured for him to begin his segment.

"Mars is remarkable," he said, then made an adjustment to his phrasing without explicitly acknowledging it as correction. "Not remarkable for its strangeness or alienness—those are the qualities we expected. What's actually striking is the consistency. The physics hold exactly as predicted. The atmospheric models match observed conditions. The geological formations align with our understanding of planetary processes. That consistency is... reassuring."

Reassuring.

He felt steadier once the word was vocalized, once he'd given permission to himself and the distant audience to find comfort in predictability, in the way Mars behaved according to laws that could be understood and calculated.

Okoye lifted her gaze directly to the camera lens when Mara indicated it was her turn, making eye contact with the future viewers who would see this recording, whoever they turned out to be.

"As a physician," she began, her voice steady and professional, "you learn very early to work within constraints. Limited resources are a constant. High stakes are the norm rather than the exception. You develop the ability to prioritize care effectively, to make difficult decisions under pressure. Decisions that preserve—"

A pause.

Less than a second in duration. Probably too brief to register as significant in the final edit.

Enormous in subjective experience.

Her throat closed momentarily around the word she'd been about to say. *Life.* Single. Singular. The preservation of individual life as the ultimate medical imperative.

"—to preserve lives," she finished, making the word plural, making it about population rather than person, about statistical outcomes rather than individual fates.

The recovery was smooth enough. Professional. Practiced. Mara's hands remained steady on the camera controls, did not flinch or adjust to acknowledge the momentary disruption. Chen noted the variance—he was trained to notice such things, deviations from expected patterns—but did not annotate it, did not draw attention to the slip.

Rourke followed, taking his position in frame when Mara gestured. He still didn't know what to do with his hands, despite multiple practice sessions. They felt wrong at his sides, wrong folded across his chest, wrong clasped in front of him. He settled for letting them hang naturally and tried not to think about it.

"Being here makes you think about scale," he said, speaking the words he'd prepared but finding them more true than he'd expected when he wrote them. "About how small we are as individuals. How vast this undertaking is. Every system matters. Every connection. Every component has to function because there's no room for failure when you're this far from any kind of backup or support."

His eyes flicked once—briefly, involuntarily—to the edge of frame, toward the direction Mara had already excluded from the composition. Toward the medical wing corridor that wasn't being documented.

Chen added, unprompted, continuing a thought that seemed to demand completion: "Redundancy matters tremendously. Verification protocols. Overlapping systems. You design in backups because you can't afford to rely on a single point of failure. Everything critical needs multiple pathways to completion."

No one had asked him to elaborate. No one had signaled that additional technical detail was needed.

He continued anyway, the words arriving faster, more urgent: "It's about collective effort. Process discipline. Trust in the systems and in each other. Precision becomes a form of shelter when you're this isolated, this dependent on everything functioning exactly as designed."

His voice carried something that wasn't quite desperation but approached it—the need to believe that what he was saying was true, that precision and redundancy actually protected against the kinds of failures that mattered most.

Hale delivered the closing statement, bringing the testimony back to the inspirational framework that mission communications preferred.

"This mission expands the boundaries of what's possible," he said, the phrasing lifted almost verbatim from approved messaging guidelines. "For science, certainly. For exploration and discovery. But ultimately for humanity—for our species' capacity to extend our presence beyond Earth. We're honored to carry this responsibility forward on behalf of everyone who made it possible."

Then, with the practiced delivery of someone who'd said these words many times in training: "For all mankind."

The recording indicator dimmed. The camera powered down with a soft electronic sigh.

No one applauded. No one exhaled with the release of tension that might have suggested the recording session had been a performance rather than authentic testimony. No one acknowledged that they'd just participated in creating content rather than simply reporting facts.

Rourke stepped out of frame first, his boots loud against the deck plating in the sudden silence, the sound aggressive in a way he probably didn't intend.

Chen remained where he was, eyes still fixed on the darkened camera lens as if waiting for a prompt that had not arrived, as if the machine might ask follow-up questions that would give him another chance to get the explanation right.

Okoye began to form a sentence—something about accuracy or completeness or the gap between what they'd said and what was true—and lost it before the words could organize themselves into coherent expression.

"It was fine," Hale said too quickly, filling the silence before it could become uncomfortable. "Clean delivery. Clear messaging. They'll receive it well."

He was still performing—not for the camera now, but for the crew. Maintaining commander's optimism, projecting confidence that would help them move past the discomfort of having just reduced their experience to talking points.

Mara saved the recording files with efficient keystrokes. Tagged them according to the classification system that determined how content would be processed and distributed.

PRIORITY: URGENT

CATEGORY: HISTORICAL

CLASSIFICATION: MISSION SUCCESS

The automated upload system accepted the files without comment or verification, beginning the compression and transmission sequence that would send their testimony across millions of kilometers to reach Earth approximately nine minutes later.

On the communications console nearby, telemetry from CONCORDIA refreshed at its scheduled interval—ninety-three-minute orbital periods producing regular data packets. The status line for Crew Member Six remained unchanged from the previous update and the update before that.

Patient status: stable.

Modified Care Protocol: active.

Orbital watch: maintained.

The word *stable* held its position in the status display, green indicator confirming that all parameters remained within acceptable ranges.

And because *stable* held, because the numbers continued to report nominal status, everything else held too. The mission timeline. The surface operations schedule. The narrative they'd just performed for the camera.

All of it sustained by that single word, by the framework's determination that current conditions met the definition of acceptable persistence.

Mara stared at the status display for several seconds after the others had dispersed to their assigned rest periods or work stations.

Stable.

The word that meant Jonah wasn't getting worse.

The word that also meant he wasn't getting better.

The word that converted indefinite suspension into achievement, that transformed maintenance into care.

The word that made everything they'd just said to the camera technically accurate while remaining fundamentally dishonest.

She closed the display and returned to her own quarters, where the unindexed archive waited—the footage that showed hesitation instead of confidence, the timestamps that revealed editing, the evidence that the official record was being optimized into a version of events that served institutional needs rather than preserving actual truth.

They had just performed for Earth. Had delivered the narrative that would be analyzed and archived and taught.

And somewhere in orbit, maintained by automated systems and pharmaceutical protocols, Jonah persisted in the state they'd defined as acceptable so that everything else could proceed.

Stable.

The word held.

And because it held, they could continue pretending that what they'd said to the camera was true.

CHAPTER 13
ECHO

THE REPLY from Earth arrived threaded into the day's routine operations—no priority alert, no urgent notification demanding immediate attention. Just a clock increment on the communications display, a queued data packet downloading during a scheduled transmission window, a quiet confirmation that their recorded performance had been received, processed, and approved.

Mara waited until they were all inside the habitat—helmets removed and stored in suitport lockers, pressure suit seals checked and verified, everyone breathing the same recycled air again—before she opened the transmission and displayed its contents on the common area screen.

It was a compilation rather than a direct response. A curated package designed for crew morale and public relations rather than operational communication.

Clipped video reactions from mission control personnel, their responses carefully selected and edited. News headlines from major outlets, the typography clean and professional. Quotes extracted from longer articles, formatted for maximum impact.

HUMANITY TAKES ITS FIRST STEPS ON MARS

CREW PRAISED FOR EXCEPTIONAL UNITY AND SACRIFICE

ARES-1 MISSION: A MODEL FOR FUTURE DEEP SPACE OPERATIONS

A video segment played automatically—Hale's closing line from their recorded testimony, the "For all mankind" phrase replayed twice in succession before the feed advanced to the next clip. The repetition transformed statement into slogan, meaning into marketing. Something you could repeat without thinking about what it meant, without examining what it cost.

Okoye stood behind Mara's shoulder, watching the compilation cycle through its curated highlights. "They liked it," she said, the observation flat, emotionally neutral.

"Yes," Mara replied, her tone carrying something that might have been bitterness or might have been simple recognition. "They loved it. Exactly what they wanted."

Chen glanced at the screen once, processed what he saw, and looked away. "They're calling it courage," he said quietly. "Making difficult decisions under impossible circumstances. That's the framing they've chosen."

Rourke made a sound that wasn't quite laughter, wasn't quite a cough. Something caught halfway between recognition and revulsion. "They always do. Convert choices into virtues. Make necessity look like valor."

Hale entered the common area last, saw what was displayed on screen, and maintained his commander's composure. Did not flinch or react visibly to seeing their testimony transformed into public narrative.

"They're requesting follow-up content," he said, reading the attached communication that accompanied the compilation. "Additional recorded segments. Individual crew member reflections on the experience. Longer-form interview responses to submitted questions."

"They want more of the same," Rourke said.

"They want continuity," Hale corrected, providing the institutional framing. "Narrative momentum. Sustained public engagement with the mission."

Mara scrolled through the compilation materials, watching the automated presentation cycle through its components. An animation loaded near the end—professionally produced, visually polished, simplified for broad audience consumption. Five stylized figures stepping onto a red planetary surface. Five silhouettes against an alien sky.

Five.

Mara's voice stayed low but carried clearly in the habitat's confined space. "They've already edited him out of the story."

The words landed in the middle of the room like a physical object.

Okoye closed her eyes. Chen turned away completely, facing the viewport where Mars turned overhead. Rourke's jaw muscles tightened visibly, tendons standing out against the skin of his neck.

"They don't know," Hale said, the defense automatic, rehearsed. "The public doesn't have access to detailed crew manifests. The simplified graphics are just—"

"No," Mara interrupted, her voice still quiet but carrying absolute certainty. "They know exactly what we gave them. Five crew members visible in the footage. Five voices in the testimony. Five people performing the narrative of collective achievement. We handed them the story they wanted, and they're using it exactly as intended."

Hale looked at the looping animation—five figures, endlessly stepping onto Mars, the cycle repeating without acknowledgment of anyone absent. "Public narrative stabilizes quickly," he said, offering the explanation that had been drilled into them during media training. "It has to. Complex stories fragment. Simplified versions achieve consensus."

"Or the narrative fractures," Okoye said, opening her eyes but not looking at the screen. "And fragmented narratives undermine institutional credibility."

"And if the narrative fractures," Hale continued, completing the logic they'd all been taught, "everything becomes contested instead of learned. Questioned instead of accepted. The framework breaks down when people start examining individual cases instead of accepting general principles."

Rourke crossed his arms across his chest, the gesture defensive, protective. "Maybe it should fracture. Maybe examination is exactly what these situations need instead of simplified lessons and tidy conclusions."

Silence filled the habitat's recycled air. No one moved to dismiss Rourke's statement. No one moved to endorse it either.

The communication system chimed with an incoming attachment—additional materials appended to the compilation. Interview prompts, suggested discussion topics, themes mission control wanted emphasized in future communications. Human-interest angles: coping with isolation, building trust among crew members, the nature of sacrifice in service of larger goals.

The language was so carefully polished it felt pre-owned, as if these exact phrases had been used before for other missions, other crews, other situations that needed to be converted into teachable moments.

Mara said it flatly, without inflection: "We're an object lesson now. Case study material for training modules and policy discussions. The crew that made hard choices and succeeded despite adversity."

The description wasn't wrong. It was accurate in the way that made accuracy feel like violence.

Okoye stood abruptly, the movement sudden enough to draw everyone's attention. She walked toward the habitat corridor that led to the pressurized connection with the DAV, which connected to CONCORDIA through the docking interface.

"Where are you going?" Hale asked.

"Medical check," she said without turning around. "Orbital telemetry shows it's time."

She went to the medical bay aboard CONCORDIA without requesting permission, without explaining why physical presence was necessary when remote monitoring provided all relevant data.

Jonah's vitals displayed on the isolation bay monitors exactly as they had during the previous check, and the check before that. Stable. All parameters within the ranges the Modified Care Protocol specified as acceptable. The machines monitoring him were calm, untroubled by the consistency, faithful to their programming.

"They're proud of us," Okoye said softly, speaking to someone who might or might not be able to hear, who might or might not be conscious enough to process language. "Earth. Mission control. The public. They say we demonstrated exceptional teamwork. They say we trusted each other when it mattered most."

Her voice thinned, the professional control wavering. "I don't know how to make that sentence true. I don't know how trust exists in a framework where the only choice was the choice we made."

She stopped short of touching him, hand extended toward the transparent barrier but not making contact. The physical separation remained absolute. The barrier held.

She stood there for several minutes, watching the steady rise and fall of his chest, the mechanical regularity of breathing that was partly his and partly the ventilator's.

Then she returned to the surface habitat without having accomplished anything measurable, without having changed anything that the remote monitoring couldn't have handled.

Back in the habitat's common area, Hale had drafted a polite response to Earth's request for additional content—acknowledging the interest, expressing willingness to contribute, but requesting a brief delay to focus on immediate scientific objectives during this critical phase of surface operations.

He saved it as a draft document. Did not finalize it. Did not transmit it.

Delay felt like restraint. Like the only form of resistance available. Like protection against something he couldn't quite articulate.

Outside the habitat, beyond the reinforced walls and protective berms, Mars continued its rotation. Dust lifted in the far distance—visible as a faint haze on the horizon, nothing urgent, nothing threatening to their operations.

Just consequence moving through thin air. Cause and effect playing out over geological timescales that made human decisions feel both infinitely significant and utterly meaningless.

Their words were no longer theirs.

The testimony they'd recorded, the narrative they'd performed, the story they'd told about teamwork and sacrifice and difficult decisions— all of it belonged to the mission now. To the institution. To the framework that would preserve and study and teach their example to future crews facing similar situations.

The machinery had absorbed them completely.

And somewhere in orbit, maintained by systems they'd helped design, Jonah persisted in the state they'd defined as acceptable so that the mission could succeed, so that the narrative could remain simple, so that five figures could step onto Mars instead of six.

Orbit: Unobserved

The medical bay lighting shifted without announcement or visible cause, transitioning from the standard operational intensity to a lower evening-cycle setting. The change was automated, programmed to simulate circadian rhythms that no longer corresponded to any natural day-night cycle.

Jonah's pupils responded automatically to the reduced illumination, contracting appropriately, biological reflex functioning despite the pharmaceutical suppression of higher cognitive processes.

For several minutes—perhaps longer, time perception was unreliable in his fragmented state—he was awake.

Fully awake.

Actually conscious rather than existing in the managed semi-awareness the protocol normally maintained.

The clarity startled him more than any physical sensation could have. His mind felt sharp, focused, capable of forming complete thoughts that connected to other thoughts in logical sequences. Not the fragmentary, dissociated awareness that had become his normal state, but genuine consciousness.

He could feel everything with precise awareness. The restraints. The IV line. The monitoring leads. The weight of the blanket. The temperature of recycled air. The subtle vibration of CONCORDIA's systems transmitted through the medical cot's frame.

He could hear the ship as discrete systems operating in concert. The circulation fans. The ventilator's cycle. The faint hum of power. The occasional click of automated adjustments.

CONCORDIA.

He was alone aboard the mothership.

They were on the surface now. All five of them. Making history while he monitored orbital systems and breathed and persisted within acceptable parameters.

He knew this with absolute certainty, though he couldn't explain how.

He tried to speak.

Nothing emerged.

He did not try again.

The clarity began to fade—pharmaceutical balance reasserting itself, consciousness dimming back toward the managed state.

Before awareness dissolved completely, one thought arrived fully formed:

They made it.

Not resentment. Not abandonment.

Just recognition that the mission had succeeded, that the choice had produced the intended outcome, that his conversion into infrastructure had enabled the achievement.

He was glad.

The protocol had done its work perfectly. Had stripped away the emotional framework that would have recognized this gladness as evidence of how thoroughly he'd been broken.

Jonah's eyes closed.

Full consciousness receded.

And in the isolation bay aboard CONCORDIA, Jonah returned to the state the framework called stable.

Content.

Maintained.

Glad to have helped.

Unaware that gladness itself was the final optimization.

CHAPTER 14

INQUIRY

THE FIRST QUESTION arrived disguised as concern.

Not accusation. Not investigation. Concern—the institutional variety that came wrapped in professional courtesy and bureaucratic procedure.

REQUEST: CLARIFICATION

CATEGORY: MEDICAL OVERSIGHT

PRIORITY: STANDARD

The priority classification was itself a message. *Standard* meant this was routine, expected, nothing to worry about. It also meant they couldn't ignore it, couldn't delay responding, couldn't treat it as optional.

Hale read the transmission twice before forwarding it to the crew, studying the phrasing for implications that might not be immediately obvious, for subtext buried in what appeared to be straightforward administrative language.

They gathered standing in the surface habitat's briefing space rather than sitting at the galley table, as if chairs implied a comfort they hadn't earned, as if sitting would suggest they approached this casually. Mars light cut in low through the dome viewport, the sun tracking its shallow arc across the Martian sky, catching suspended dust particles and turning them briefly pale—almost gold—as if the planet had temporarily mis-registered its own color palette.

Mara brought the formal request up on the shared display, expanding the attachment so everyone could read the full text simultaneously.

In light of increased public interest in the ARES-1 mission and its historic achievements, medical oversight requests confirmation that internal reporting protocols remain fully aligned with external communications. This verification is standard procedure for missions of significant public visibility.

Oversight. Not a person's name, not a specific department. Just "oversight"—human decision-makers hidden behind a hybrid interface, institutional proxies trained to sound neutral, to avoid personal accountability while maintaining administrative authority.

"Alignment," Chen said, reading the key word that carried most of the message's weight. "That's not actually a question. That's an instruction disguised as verification."

"It's a warning," Mara replied, her archivist's training making her sensitive to how language functioned institutionally. "They're telling us they've noticed potential inconsistencies. Giving us an opportunity to correct the record before they make it official."

A second paragraph populated on the screen as the document fully rendered:

Please confirm that no material changes have occurred in crew medical status since the last comprehensive transmission. If changes have occurred, please provide updated documentation using approved reporting frameworks.

"Material," Rourke said, isolating the word that did most of the work. "Undefined on purpose. They're not specifying what counts as material because they want us to define it ourselves, to reveal what we think needs reporting."

"They want consistency," Hale said, providing the institutional interpretation. "Documentation that doesn't create contradictions or raise questions that undermine the public narrative."

"With the story," Mara corrected, making the distinction explicit. "Not consistency with facts. Consistency with the version of events they've already started circulating."

Another attachment unfolded on screen—a checklist with expandable sections, each category representing a potential area of scrutiny:

Timeline confirmation – Verify that all significant medical events occurred as previously reported

Care protocol activation criteria – Document decision factors that triggered protocol implementation

Resource impact summary – Quantify how protocol adjustments affected mission resource allocation

Consent documentation – Confirm appropriate authorization procedures were followed

The final category pulsed faintly on the display, highlighted automatically by whatever algorithm determined emphasis priorities.

Consent documentation.

"They want the paper trail," Chen said, understanding immediately what the emphasis meant. "Physical evidence that everything was done according to established procedures. Signed authorizations, logged approvals, documented decision points."

"They want defensible language," Rourke added. "Words that can withstand external review. Phrasing that converts moral ambiguity into administrative compliance."

Okoye stared at the screen without speaking, her focus apparently on the words but her awareness elsewhere. Jonah's telemetry scrolled in a minimized panel at the edge of the shared display—orbital data relayed from CONCORDIA with the inevitable communication lag, arriving clean and stable, delayed by both distance and the processing protocols that filtered raw data into presentable summaries.

"They're asking about consent," she said finally, her voice quiet but carrying clearly in the habitat's confined space. "Specifically. That's what this inquiry actually addresses."

"We documented group consensus," Hale replied, the response automatic, rehearsed. "Five crew members present, five confirmations recorded. The framework recognizes collective authorization for mission-critical medical decisions."

"That's not consent," Okoye said, each word emerging with deliberate precision. "Consensus is what the group decides. Consent is what the individual agrees to. Those aren't the same category."

"It's what the framework allows," Hale said, and the statement hung between them—not quite justification, not quite acknowledgment of inadequacy. Simply description of the boundaries within which they'd operated.

They assembled the response carefully over the next hour, working through each checklist category with methodical attention to detail. Dates aligned with previously submitted reports, ensuring no contradictions emerged between different documentation versions. Phrasing nested carefully inside existing protocol language, using established terminology rather than introducing new descriptive frameworks that might invite scrutiny. Nothing new was introduced that might expand the scope of inquiry. Nothing was contradicted that might suggest unreliability in previous reporting.

The work felt less like answering questions than reinforcing a structure already in place, like building buttresses around something that was fundamentally unstable but needed to appear solid for institutional purposes.

Okoye monitored Jonah's telemetry feed as they worked, the orbital data updating at regular intervals. Vitals unchanged from the previous cycle. Respiratory rate steady. Neural activity contained within the narrow bands the protocol specified. Parameters all holding within acceptable ranges.

Stable.

The word hovered between screens, applied at a distance of 900 kilometers and nine-tenths of a second of communication lag, describing a state that everyone understood meant something different from what the word suggested.

When the draft response was complete—all checklist items addressed, all documentation cross-referenced, all language vetted for consistency with the approved narrative—Hale paused with the cursor positioned over the SEND authorization.

"Any objections?" he asked, following the protocol for collective decision-making even though everyone in the habitat understood this was formality rather than actual choice. "Last chance to revise before this becomes part of the permanent record."

No one spoke.

The silence extended long enough to become meaningful, to suggest that absence of objection wasn't quite the same as approval, that consensus achieved through exhaustion might not constitute genuine agreement.

Hale sent it.

STATUS: DELIVERED

The confirmation appeared immediately—their response accepted into the institutional communication system, queued for transmission during the next Earth relay window, already archived in multiple redundant databases that would preserve this version of events for future analysis.

For a moment after the transmission confirmed, nothing happened. The habitat's ambient systems hummed. Mars rotated fractionally beyond the viewport. Time continued its measured progression.

Then the automated response arrived, faster than normal human processing would have allowed, suggesting this reply had been pre-formatted, waiting for their submission before populating with specific details:

FOLLOW-UP REVIEW SCHEDULED

FORMAT: ASYNCHRONOUS INTERVIEW

REQUESTED PARTICIPANTS: COMMANDER HALE, MEDICAL OFFICER OKOYE

TIMELINE: NEXT COMMUNICATION CYCLE

Okoye felt the room tilt slightly—not actually, the habitat's structural integrity remained perfect—but subjectively, as if her inner ear's sense of vertical had momentarily failed. The environmental control systems corrected temperature and pressure fluctuations without comment, maintaining parameters that prevented physical instability even as psychological stability degraded.

"They're separating our answers," Chen said, recognizing the significance of individual rather than collective interviews. "Comparing our statements for consistency. Looking for gaps between how we each describe what happened."

"To compare," Mara added, making the implication explicit. "To identify discrepancies that might suggest the consensus wasn't as solid as we've reported. That someone might tell a different version under individual questioning."

"When?" Okoye asked, though the display had already provided the timeline. The question was reflex, buying time to process implications.

"Next cycle," Hale confirmed. "Approximately twenty-three hours from now based on orbital communication windows."

Okoye did not promise to tell the truth during the interview. The sentence formed in her mind but didn't reach vocalization.

She did not promise to protect the crew, to maintain the unified narrative, to subordinate her individual perspective to collective necessity.

Those sentences didn't arrive either.

What remained unsaid accumulated mass, became presence through absence.

The communication channel closed automatically after the standard timeout period.

For several seconds after the screen went dark, no one moved. No one spoke. Outside the viewport, Mars rotated fractionally, its ancient geology indifferent to human inquiry, indifferent to whether the questions being asked would reveal truth or simply reinforce the structures that made truth irrelevant.

Hale cleared his throat—a small sound, barely audible, but enough to break the silence.

"We should prepare for the interview protocols," he said, commander's voice returning, professional tone reasserting itself. "Review what we've documented. Ensure our individual responses align with the collective record we've built."

Rourke nodded once—acknowledgment without enthusiasm.

Chen reopened the checklist on his personal tablet, already beginning the work of cross-referencing their submitted response against previous documentation, looking for potential inconsistencies that the inquiry might target.

Mara minimized the display and returned to her station, but not before noting the timestamp, the participants list, the format specifications— all the metadata that would help her understand how this inquiry fit into larger institutional patterns.

Okoye returned her attention to Jonah's orbital telemetry feed, watching the data scroll past. Already delayed by the time it took signals to travel between surface and orbit. Already filtered through processing protocols that converted raw sensor readings into simplified status reports.

Stable.

The inquiry had crossed a threshold. Had moved from passive acceptance of their reported narrative to active verification, from trusting institutional actors to checking their work, from celebrating their achievement to questioning their methods.

This wasn't reassurance.

It was ownership.

The framework was reclaiming them, pulling them back into the machinery that had created the conditions for their impossible choice, preparing to document and study and ultimately absorb what they'd done into the institutional knowledge base that would guide future crews facing similar situations.

They had become case study material.

And the inquiry would ensure that the case study told the right story.

Orbit: Unobserved

The medical bay lighting shifted without announcement or warning notification, transitioning from standard operational intensity to the lower evening-cycle setting according to automated schedules that simulated Earth-normal circadian patterns despite their complete irrelevance to anyone's actual biological needs.

Jonah's pupils responded automatically to the illumination change, contracting to accommodate the reduced light input.

For several minutes—perhaps longer, he had lost any reliable means of measuring duration—he was awake.

Fully awake.

Actually, genuinely conscious in the way he'd been before the protocol, before the pharmaceutical suppression, before his existence had been reduced to narrow maintenance channels.

The clarity startled him more profoundly than any physical sensation could have.

He could feel everything with precise, undulled awareness. The restraints crossing his chest and hips, not uncomfortable exactly but undeniably present. The IV line in his arm, foreign object piercing skin. The catheter, the monitoring leads, the ventilator mask. The weight of the thermal blanket across his legs. The ambient temperature of recycled air moving through the isolation bay.

He could hear the ship—not as background white noise, but as a collection of discrete systems operating in concert, each contributing its signature sound to CONCORDIA's mechanical symphony. The circulation fans. The ventilator's regular cycle. The faint hum of power distribution. The occasional click of automated equipment making micro-adjustments.

CONCORDIA.

He was alone aboard the mothership.

The certainty arrived without drama, without emotional weight, just recognition of observable fact supported by sensory evidence and logical inference.

They were on the surface now. All five of them. Conducting the surface operations he'd helped plan during the outbound journey, collecting geological samples, documenting everything, making the discoveries that would justify the entire mission.

He knew this with absolute confidence though he couldn't explain the source of that knowledge. No one had told him explicitly. No announcement had been made. But the knowledge felt settled, finished, incontrovertible.

He tested his voice, attempting to speak.

Tried to form words. To say something that would confirm his presence, that would mark this moment of clarity as real rather than some pharmaceutical artifact.

Nothing emerged from his throat. The neural signals transmitted but arrived at muscles too degraded to execute voluntary commands.

He did not try again. The effort required exceeded the value of confirmation.

Instead, he listened to the habitat's ambient sounds, waiting for the moment when someone would enter the medical bay, would adjust a setting, would speak his name and acknowledge his presence as something more than monitored parameters.

The moment did not arrive.

Time stretched, contracted, lost coherent definition. Seconds might have been minutes. Minutes might have been hours. The usual markers that made temporal measurement possible had become unreliable.

At some point—he couldn't specify when—a memory surfaced with unusual clarity: his hands moving across a control console, anticipating a system fault before it announced itself through alerts, redistributing load across backup pathways, preventing cascade failure through proactive intervention rather than reactive response.

He smiled.

The expression felt unfamiliar on his face, muscles responding to an emotional impulse that had been absent for so long the physical manifestation seemed foreign.

If the systems needed him, they would call. Would trigger alerts that required human judgment to resolve.

They did not.

CONCORDIA operated flawlessly. All automated systems functioned within design parameters. The orbital mechanics were stable. Power generation balanced. Life support maintained. Communications relays operated on schedule.

His presence was unnecessary.

Eventually, inevitably, the clarity began to recede. Pharmaceutical balance reasserting itself. Consciousness narrowing again to the channel the Modified Care Protocol allowed, closing down the full awareness that had briefly surfaced.

Before it closed completely, before the managed state reclaimed him, one final thought surfaced—calm, almost satisfied:

They're doing fine without me.

The recognition carried no bitterness. No resentment. Just acknowledgment that the mission had successfully optimized around his absence, that his conversion into infrastructure had enabled rather than hindered their achievement.

The system agreed with his assessment.

It recorded nothing. No alert triggered. No status change logged. His moment of full consciousness left no trace in any database, generated no documentation that would suggest the protocol's suppression had temporarily failed.

As far as the institutional record was concerned, Jonah remained exactly what the framework defined him as:

Stable.

Maintained.

Unaware that his gladness at their success was itself the protocol's final achievement.

CHAPTER 15

DIVERGENCE

GROUND'S RESPONSE to their inquiry answers did not arrive as accusation or challenge.

It arrived as gratitude.

Thank you for your cooperation with the review process.

Your responses are currently under evaluation by the oversight committee.

No action is required at this time.

No action—for now. The qualifier hung invisible in the white space after the message, implied rather than stated, a threat constructed from absence rather than presence.

Hale forwarded the transmission to the crew without adding commentary. No one replied to acknowledge receiving it. The words performed their work without needing explicit acknowledgment, reshaping the psychological landscape simply by existing.

Okoye did not consciously decide to stop speaking to Jonah during medical monitoring sessions.

The words simply failed to arrive when she reached for them. At first the silence felt temporary—attributed to fatigue, to the cognitive drain of managing multiple systems simultaneously, to the unnatural communication lag that made conversation across 900 kilometers feel disconnected and artificial. But the silence held, settled, became the new default. When she noticed herself relying entirely on the protocol's automated systems to manage his care, allowing the framework to speak on her behalf through algorithmic adjustments and logged parameters, she did not correct the pattern.

She documented instead.

She initiated the next scheduled medical session from the surface habitat's medical console exactly on time. Not early, which might suggest excessive concern. Not late, which might indicate avoidance. Precisely when the schedule specified.

The communications link established automatically. Lighting in CONCORDIA's medical bay adjusted remotely to examination levels. Interface displays activated. Jonah's image resolved on her screen as it had for days now, weeks now, time blurring into undifferentiated maintenance cycles.

Stable.

The status indicator glowed green. All parameters within acceptable ranges.

She did not greet him. Did not announce her presence or explain what she was about to do. The protocol didn't require verbal communication with patients in managed care states. Efficiency suggested omitting unnecessary elements.

She went to the parameter console first, her attention on the data rather than the person the data represented. Scrolled through threshold settings. Confirmed automated adjustments had executed correctly. Verified resource consumption remained within projected margins. Logged routine maintenance completions.

The sequence moved through her hands with practiced ease, each action following logically from the previous one. Efficient. Clean. Defensible if reviewed.

Jonah's image on the video feed lagged a fraction of a second behind her input commands—communication delay plus processing latency producing visible desynchronization. The lag flattened his expression, softened any motion into something ambiguous. He might have been sleeping. He might have been watching her through the camera. He might have been conscious or unconscious, aware or absent. The system's monitoring couldn't distinguish with certainty, and the protocol didn't require certainty at his current care level.

She waited after completing the verification sequence, hands poised above the interface, as if waiting for some part of herself to object to what was happening, to surface with resistance or doubt or moral clarity.

Nothing happened.

Then she made a minor adjustment to his pharmaceutical regimen—permitted by the protocol, actually recommended by the system's optimization algorithms, fully supported by the framework's resource management logic. A fractional reduction in one of the supplemental medications. Not the core sedation that maintained his managed state, but an auxiliary support element. A five percent decrease that would save resources without significantly impacting outcomes as the protocol defined them.

Logged as optimization. Justified as efficiency improvement. The system accepted the change immediately, recalculating projected consumption and updating resource availability projections without protest or warning.

Okoye recognized, in one clean and terrible instant of clarity, that the work she was performing had shifted from care into something else. From healing into maintenance. From maintenance into management. From management into execution.

The word arrived fully formed in her mind: *execution*. Not in the sense of killing—the protocol was keeping him alive, maintaining all vital functions within specified parameters. But execution in the sense of carrying out instructions, implementing predetermined sequences, performing tasks that someone else had designed for purposes that extended beyond the individual being acted upon.

She was executing the framework's logic. Implementing its priorities. Converting its abstract principles into concrete pharmaceutical adjustments that would optimize resource allocation across the mission's duration.

She did not look at Jonah's image on the video feed while she confirmed the adjustment.

When the modification completed—system accepting the new parameters, automated pumps adjusting delivery rates, monitoring protocols updating expected ranges—she remained still longer than the procedure required. Not for him. Not to offer any form of acknowledgment or apology. But to see if anything in her would rise in protest, if some residual ethical core would surface with objection or resistance or horror at what she'd become capable of doing.

Nothing did.

The adjustment felt normal. Reasonable. Justified by the framework that she'd agreed to operate within, that she'd helped implement, that she'd never actually refused despite whatever reservations she'd expressed during the initial decision process.

She recorded the session as complete. Added a brief clinical note: "Protocol adjustments implemented per optimization recommendations. All parameters remain stable. No intervention required."

The language felt comfortable now. Safe. Protective of her in ways that honesty wouldn't be.

Later that sol, during the common area meal period that served as their primary collective gathering time, Mara noticed the timestamp in the shared medical logs while reviewing system summaries. She expanded the entry, examining what had been recorded.

No free text beyond the clinical summary. No annotations about Jonah's state or condition. No observations about whether he'd shown any signs of awareness or response. Just data: parameters verified, adjustments logged, optimization implemented.

The log read like maintenance documentation for equipment rather than care notes for a person.

Chen saw the entry too when he performed his routine cross-check of resource utilization against projections. He said nothing about what he observed. Didn't comment on the adjustment or question the optimization. He reran the numbers independently, verified alignment between Okoye's actions and the protocol's recommendations—dates consistent, actions justified within the framework's logic, thresholds respected exactly as specified.

Everything checked. Everything aligned. The system validated itself.

Rourke passed the medical console during his evening systems inspection route and did not slow his pace, did not pause to check the displays, did not inquire about Jonah's status. The medical wing had become someone else's responsibility, someone else's burden, someone else's problem to solve or not solve as the framework dictated.

Hale reviewed the evening mission status report before initiating his sleep cycle.

Medical: Stable.

Crew: Operational.

Mission: Nominal.

The language felt easier now than it had weeks ago when these same words had required conscious effort to accept, when calling things "nominal" had felt like violence against truth.

Repetition had worn the edges smooth. The words no longer cut when he said them.

Okoye did not initiate contact early during the next scheduled medical session. Did not deviate from the prescribed timing. Did not add any elements the protocol didn't specify.

She followed schedule. Followed sequence. Verified parameters. Logged completions.

No greeting. No hesitation. No speech directed at the person whose care she was managing.

Once, without consciously intending to vocalize, she heard herself say aloud: "Within tolerance."

The phrase startled her—not because it was inaccurate, but because she'd spoken it unconsciously, as if the framework's language had become her internal voice, replacing whatever thoughts she'd once formulated in her own words.

She stopped. Listened to the habitat's ambient hum. Waited for some follow-up thought to arrive, some completion of the sentence that would reveal what she'd meant or what she'd been about to say.

Nothing else followed.

The phrase stood alone: *Within tolerance.*

That was the entire thought. Complete. Sufficient. Nothing more needed saying.

Outside the habitat, beyond the reinforced walls and protective berms, a localized dust front passed over their position without incident or drama. The kind of minor atmospheric disturbance that happened constantly on Mars, that the habitat's systems were designed to ignore unless it escalated beyond defined thresholds.

Solar power output dipped slightly. The reactor compensated automatically. Power distribution remained balanced. Structural anchors held steady under the marginal load increase. No alert fired. No threshold crossed. No human intervention required.

Inside the habitat, the crew's routines absorbed the environmental change without acknowledgment. Dust outside, stability inside. Mars continuing its processes, humans continuing theirs, both operating according to physical laws that didn't require permission or approval.

Something had ended during these cycles, during this gradual progression from initial decision to sustained implementation.

Not Jonah's life—he remained alive by every biological and legal definition, maintained by systems that would continue functioning until explicitly instructed otherwise.

What had ended was Okoye's objection.

The resistance she'd felt initially. The moral clarity that had made the decision difficult rather than automatic. The part of her that had wanted to refuse, to say no, to choose differently even knowing that different choices led to different forms of failure.

That had ended.

Not through dramatic collapse or sudden capitulation. Through attrition. Through accumulated small acceptances of what the framework defined as necessary. Through the daily practice of performing care that wasn't actually care, through the routine of maintaining life that wasn't actually living, through the efficiency of optimization that prioritized mission over person until the distinction felt natural rather than monstrous.

The system did not require her agreement—it never had. Systems could function regardless of whether the people operating them believed in their logic or endorsed their conclusions.

The system only required her compliance.

And now—cleanly, remotely, efficiently, without conscious resistance or explicit surrender—

She gave it.

Not because she'd been forced. Not because alternatives had been foreclosed. But because the framework had successfully reshaped what felt possible to think, to feel, to object to.

She had been optimized.

The pharmaceutical adjustments she made to Jonah's regimen were optimizations.

The reduction in supplemental care was optimization.

The conversion of person into parameter was optimization.

And her own transformation from physician who healed into technician who maintained was optimization.

The protocol had done its work perfectly.

On both of them.

CHAPTER 16
VARIANCE

THE INTERVIEW DID NOT FEEL like an interrogation.

That was the design.

Okoye sat alone in a neutral space within the surface habitat—a small room typically used for private communications with Earth, now repurposed for this session. Walls painted matte gray to minimize visual distraction. Corners softened by architectural design to reduce psychological pressure. Lighting calibrated to reduce eye strain while maintaining alertness. As she settled into the chair, the interface adjusted itself automatically: audio levels smoothed to eliminate acoustic harshness, posture recognition sensors detected her spine alignment and adjusted seat support to maintain ergonomic tolerance.

The room did not acknowledge Mars. There was no viewport allowing external visibility. No dust-filtered light penetrating from outside. No reminder of the alien environment beyond the habitat walls. Only interior balance, controlled atmosphere, human-designed comfort.

A voice appeared without accompanying image—just audio, gender-neutral in tone, professionally modulated to convey authority without aggression.

"Dr. Okoye," it said. "Thank you for your time."

Time, she thought, *had already been allocated*. This wasn't optional participation. But the phrasing suggested gratitude for voluntary cooperation, converting obligation into choice through linguistic sleight.

"This session is supplemental," the voice continued, establishing parameters. "Clarificatory in nature, not corrective. We're seeking to understand the decision-making process more completely, not to evaluate whether decisions were correct."

Clarificatory, not corrective. The distinction was intentional. Suggesting this was about understanding rather than judgment, about documentation rather than accountability.

Okoye inclined her head in acknowledgment. The gesture registered through the room's camera system—some algorithm noting her body language, categorizing her response as cooperative, compliant, appropriately deferential to institutional authority.

"We'd like to revisit the decision sequence," the voice said, moving directly into substance without further preamble. "Specifically, the reservations you expressed prior to achieving consensus."

They did not say *objections*. Did not use language that suggested actual resistance or fundamental disagreement. Just *reservations*—temporary hesitation that was eventually resolved through proper process.

"Those were documented," Okoye said, her voice sounding steadier than she felt internally. "At the time of the decision. The record contains my concerns as I stated them."

"And at present?" the voice asked. "How would you characterize those reservations now, with the benefit of additional time and perspective?"

The question arrived cleanly, without obvious emphasis or leading inflection. Its neutrality was complete, surgical. It invited her to distance herself from her earlier position, to revise her objections into something more compatible with the choice that had ultimately been made.

"At present," Okoye said, selecting each word with conscious deliberation, "the protocol is operating within its defined parameters. The outcomes have aligned with the framework's projections."

Not an answer to what she'd asked. An answer to what the voice wanted —confirmation that the system worked as designed.

A pause followed—brief, precisely measured. Long enough to register acknowledgment without creating uncomfortable silence.

"Yes," the voice said. "That aligns with current operational reporting from the medical monitoring systems."

A new prompt resolved on the display screen positioned at eye level:

IN YOUR PROFESSIONAL MEDICAL OPINION, WAS FULL CURATIVE CARE EVER A VIABLE OPTION GIVEN AVAILABLE RESOURCES?

Okoye recognized the structure immediately. The question wasn't actually about medical viability—it was about establishing boundaries. About getting her to confirm that the choice had been constrained by objective limitations rather than subjective priorities.

"Viable," she said carefully, "is a contingent term. It depends on what risks are considered acceptable."

"And in this situation," the voice pressed gently, "was the risk of full care acceptable given mission parameters?"

She waited half a second longer than conversational flow required.

The hesitation registered. Some metric somewhere noted the pause, categorized it as significance, flagged it for potential follow-up.

"Acceptability," she said, "depends on which outcome is prioritized. Full care prioritizes individual recovery. Modified care prioritizes collective survival. The framework defines which priority takes precedence under resource constraint conditions."

Another pause. Longer this time.

"That distinction is noted for the record," the voice said. "For clarity in documentation: which outcome did the crew ultimately prioritize?"

The crew.

Not *you*. Not her individual choice. The collective decision that distributed responsibility across all participants, making accountability diffuse, impossible to locate in any single person.

"Mission continuity," Okoye said.

The answer settled without resistance. She felt it lock into place like a component fitting into a pre-designed slot, confirming the shape the interview had been constructed to produce.

The voice's tone adjusted slightly—approval indistinguishable from simple acknowledgment, but carrying subtle positive reinforcement nonetheless.

"Thank you. That corresponds with the parallel accounts we've received from other crew members."

Parallel accounts. They were comparing stories, checking for consistency, verifying that everyone told the same version. Building a unified narrative from individual testimonies.

The next prompt appeared on screen, its phrasing notably gentler than the previous question:

DID YOU FEEL PRESSURED OR COERCED TO PROVIDE CONSENT FOR THE MODIFIED CARE PROTOCOL?

"No," Okoye said.

The word arrived too quickly, emerging before she'd fully processed the question's implications.

Not because the answer was complete or entirely accurate, but because its opposite—admitting to pressure or coercion—required expansion, explanation, evidence that she couldn't produce without contradicting the framework she'd already validated.

"Were your medical concerns heard and considered by the crew during the decision process?"

"Yes," she said.

They had been. That remained factually true. People had listened when she spoke. They had acknowledged her objections. That her concerns had then been subordinated to mission priorities didn't change the fact that they'd been registered.

"Do you consider the final decision to have been ethical given the circumstances and constraints you faced?"

The question tightened something behind her sternum—a physical response to moral pressure. She inhaled deliberately. The room's environmental controls responded with a fractional adjustment to oxygen flow, some algorithm detecting respiratory stress and compensating automatically.

"Ethical," she said, parsing the word carefully, "within the framework provided for making such decisions. The protocol exists because situations like this have ethical dimensions that can't be resolved through individual judgment alone. The framework provides the structure for making choices when all available options involve harm."

The voice accepted this qualification without challenge or follow-up.

"Noted. That characterization will be included in the review documentation."

A final prompt resolved on screen:

BASED ON YOUR EXPERIENCE, IS THERE ANYTHING YOU WOULD CHANGE ABOUT HOW THIS SITUATION WAS HANDLED?

Okoye held her gaze on the text longer than necessary, longer than the question warranted, studying the words as if they might reveal some hidden meaning through extended observation.

She saw Jonah's hands again—not his face, not his voice, not any personal characteristic that would make him individual rather than categorical. Just his hands, the way they had moved through CONCORDIA during the outbound journey, redistributing load before anyone asked, anticipating failures before they announced themselves, preventing problems through proactive attention that made his work invisible until he was no longer there to perform it.

How his absence now performed the same function—quietly enabling the mission to continue, making success possible through his conversion into infrastructure.

"I would," she said slowly, the answer surprising her even as she spoke it, "recommend defining operational thresholds earlier in mission planning. Establishing clearer parameters for when protocol activation becomes necessary, rather than making those determinations under acute pressure."

The answer surprised her because it was procedural rather than ethical. It suggested the problem had been timing and planning rather than the fundamental choice itself. It accepted the framework while proposing optimization—exactly the kind of feedback institutional systems wanted, the kind that reinforced rather than challenged their basic logic.

The voice did not sound surprised.

"That recommendation has been logged and will be forwarded to mission planning committees," it said. "Thank you for your candor and cooperation. Your input will contribute to improved protocols for future missions."

The interface dimmed to standby mode.

SESSION COMPLETE.

TRANSCRIPT ARCHIVED FOR REVIEW.

The room's environmental controls adjusted back to standard settings. The door unsealed with a soft pneumatic hiss.

Okoye remained seated.

Later, alone in her quarters during the designated sleep period she wasn't using for actual sleep, she mentally replayed the objections she still carried intact somewhere in her consciousness—concerns about prognosis uncertainty, about first-do-no-harm principles, about the duty to prioritize patient welfare over institutional convenience.

They arrived in her mind fully formed, articulate, unchanged from how she'd initially experienced them weeks ago when the decision was first being discussed.

But they arrived without urgency now. Like arguments prepared for a trial that had already concluded, like evidence assembled for a case that had been dismissed before it could be heard. Perfectly preserved but functionally inert.

She could feel precisely where each objection failed when tested against the framework's logic. Could identify the exact points where individual ethical intuition collided with institutional necessity and lost. Could trace how moral clarity degraded into moral ambiguity when resource constraints were introduced as variables.

She realized with uncomfortable clarity that she had begun editing herself before speaking—during the interview, during medical sessions, during any moment that might be documented and reviewed. Not editing for accuracy or truthfulness, but editing for endurance. Selecting only the thoughts that could survive institutional scrutiny. Expressing only the concerns that could be absorbed without challenging the system's fundamental assumptions.

The surviving sentences—the ones she actually voiced—were correct within the framework's terms.

They were also inert. Defanged. Optimized into harmlessness.

The system had not silenced her through overt suppression or explicit censorship.

It had done something more insidious.

It had optimized her.

Shaped her thinking through accumulated small adjustments until she could no longer distinguish between what she actually believed and what the framework permitted her to believe. Converted her objections into reservations, her resistance into alignment, her ethical clarity into procedural compliance.

She was still speaking. Still expressing concerns. Still participating in decision-making processes.

But the person speaking was no longer quite the same person who had begun this mission. That earlier version—the one who had believed individual patient welfare should take precedence over institutional priorities, who had thought some choices shouldn't be made regardless of their logical justification—had been systematically deconstructed and rebuilt according to specifications she'd never consciously agreed to.

The protocol had optimized her pharmaceutical management of Jonah's care.

And in the process, it had optimized her.

Reduced her to a function within the system. A role to be performed. A voice that could be relied upon to say the right things in the right ways at the right times.

She lay on her bunk, staring at the habitat ceiling, listening to the environmental systems hum.

Stable, she thought.

The word that described Jonah's condition.

The word that also described her own psychological state as the framework measured such things.

Stable meaning contained. Manageable. Operating within acceptable parameters.

Stable meaning no longer capable of genuine resistance.

Stable meaning optimized.

CHAPTER 17

EXPLANATIONS

THE QUESTIONS ARRIVED LABELED **FOLLOW-UP** and **OPTIONAL**, distributed across multiple communication cycles, spaced irregularly enough to feel spontaneous rather than systematic.

Polite enough in their phrasing to imply genuine choice about participation.

Precise enough in their timing and targeting to remove that choice entirely.

Hale received them one at a time, each question appearing small and manageable in isolation. But together—when he assembled them mentally, when he saw the pattern they formed—they constituted a corridor. A narrowing pathway toward a specific destination the questions were designed to reach.

The first prompt appeared during his morning status review:

Please clarify your use of the term "consensus" in previous responses. Specifically, describe the process by which individual perspectives were integrated into collective decision-making.

He read it twice, parsing the phrasing for implications, looking for the trap embedded in what appeared to be straightforward clarification.

He typed a response. Deleted it. Read the question again. Typed a different version.

All crew members were provided opportunity to voice concerns during deliberation. Concerns were considered within the context of mission constraints and available resources. Final alignment reflected shared understanding of mission priorities and unavoidable limitations.

Opportunity. Provided, not seized. Passive construction suggesting benevolent structure rather than individual agency.

Considered. Acknowledged, not necessarily acted upon.

Constraints. External forces limiting choice, absolving individual responsibility.

Alignment. Not agreement—something more passive, more inevitable. Settling into position rather than actively choosing.

He reviewed what he'd written. The language felt correct. Defensible. Each word selected for its capacity to withstand institutional scrutiny while maintaining plausible deniability about what it actually meant.

He sent it.

Another prompt followed within minutes, suggesting the responses were being processed in real-time, that someone—or something—was evaluating his answers immediately and generating follow-ups based on his specific phrasing:

Please confirm whether dissent persisted following protocol activation, or whether consensus was maintained throughout implementation.

Simpler question. Binary structure. Designed for yes/no response that would eliminate ambiguity.

No, he typed. Single word. Unambiguous.

He sent it.

Immediately, another question appeared:

Please describe specific measures taken to mitigate moral distress among crew members following the difficult decision to implement Modified Care Protocol.

Hale did not hesitate this time. The answer was well-rehearsed, had become automatic through repetition:

Crew structure, established routine, and clear command leadership provided psychological stability during a high-stress transition period. Maintaining operational focus helped crew members process the decision within a productive framework.

Stability again.

The word did what it always did: held shape under pressure, contained complexity within simple syllables, converted chaos into comprehensible category.

The questions stopped arriving after that third response.

Hale remained seated at the communications console anyway, hands poised over the interface, mentally composing answers for prompts that had not yet materialized. Explanation had become reflex—language generating itself automatically to fill potential silence before that silence could be interpreted as evasion or resistance or doubt.

He caught himself drafting a response to a question that didn't exist yet, pre-emptively justifying decisions that no one had challenged.

The realization unsettled him more than the actual interrogation had.

Chen's prompt arrived later that same cycle, during what should have been his designated rest period:

Please confirm whether your quantitative assessment of resource margins changed following protocol activation, or whether the margins remained consistent with pre-activation calculations.

He read it carefully, recognizing the precision of the phrasing, how it invited him to separate numerical accuracy from interpretive framing.

He answered with equal precision:

Numerical projections remained mathematically consistent. Interpretation of acceptable risk thresholds adjusted in response to evolving mission context and updated priority weighting.

Precision as protective cover. Mathematics as moral shield. Still.

The numbers hadn't changed. Only what the numbers were permitted to mean.

Rourke's prompt was notably briefer than the others, almost blunt in its directness:

At any point during the decision process or subsequent implementation, did you feel pressured or coerced to agree with the Modified Care Protocol activation?

He stared at the screen longer than the question warranted, longer than response efficiency required.

Pressure. Coercion. Words that implied external force, explicit threat, violation of autonomy.

None of which had occurred, technically. No one had threatened him. No consequences had been specified for dissent. The framework had simply made the alternatives clear and let physics do the rest.

He typed a single word:

No.

Sent it.

Closed the interface immediately, before any follow-up could arrive, before the question could expand into something that required more elaborate explanation.

Okoye received nothing during that cycle.

No questions. No requests for clarification. No prompts seeking additional detail.

The absence unsettled her more than active interrogation would have. Silence suggested either that her previous interview had been sufficient

—that she'd already provided everything the system needed—or that she'd been deemed unreliable, her responses too unstable to incorporate into the consolidated narrative.

She wasn't sure which possibility disturbed her more.

She stood at the medical monitoring console, running the routine check sequence on Jonah's status even though automated systems had already performed the same verification. Looking for something to do with her hands, some action that felt purposeful.

Stable.

All parameters within acceptable ranges.

Without consciously intending to vocalize, she heard herself say softly: "Within tolerance."

The phrase felt unfamiliar in her mouth despite how many times she'd read it in status reports, how many times she'd logged it in medical documentation. Hearing it spoken aloud in her own voice made it feel foreign, borrowed, as if she were reciting someone else's language.

Mara did not receive a question at all.

Instead, she received a system notification during her evening data review:

INTERNAL REVIEW UPDATE

Status: Response convergence improving across crew testimonies

Assessment: No further clarification required at this time

Archive status: Discrepancy resolution in progress

Improving—as if alignment were a measurable trend line, as if consensus could be quantified through statistical analysis of linguistic variance.

She opened the metadata summary attached to the notification, examining the analysis that someone—or some algorithm—had performed on the crew's collective responses.

Hale's responses showed narrowing variance over successive prompts, language becoming more standardized, more aligned with approved terminology.

Chen's answers remained tightly controlled throughout, minimal deviation from technical precision, mathematics providing consistent framework.

Rourke's responses were notably minimal in length, single-word confirmations where possible, avoiding elaboration that might introduce inconsistency.

Okoye's contribution was marked simply as "interview complete"—her silence after the initial session apparently interpreted as settled position rather than ongoing uncertainty.

The system liked silence, Mara realized. Silence was easy to reconcile with any narrative. Absence of contradiction could be read as agreement.

That evening, they moved through the shared habitat with careful deliberation, avoiding spontaneous interaction that might require explanation later, that might be recorded and analyzed and used to identify inconsistencies in their collective story.

Normalcy became choreography—each action performed with awareness that it might be observed, documented, incorporated into assessment of their reliability and cohesion.

They did not discuss the follow-up questions. Did not compare what they'd been asked or how they'd answered. The conversation that should have happened—coordinating stories, identifying gaps, ensuring consistency—never occurred because having that conversation would itself constitute evidence of something the system might interpret as problematic.

. . .

Later, alone in his quarters during the sleep period he wasn't using for actual rest, Hale pulled up the most recent prompt he'd received and caught himself mentally drafting yet another response despite no new question having arrived.

He stopped. Stared at the blank interface.

He realized—without particular shock, without the emotional impact the recognition should have carried—that he could explain anything now. Instantly. Fluently. Automatically.

Any decision, any outcome, any choice could be converted into defensible language that nested perfectly within institutional frameworks, that used approved terminology, that referenced established protocols, that distributed responsibility across collective structures.

That was the danger.

Not that he couldn't defend their decisions.

But that he could defend them too easily.

Because the explanations were no longer arriving to protect truth.

They were arriving to replace it.

Language had become autonomous, generating itself according to rules he'd internalized so completely he no longer noticed when he was following them. The framework had colonized his thinking to the point where he could justify anything using words that sounded reasonable, that met all formal criteria for adequate explanation, that satisfied institutional requirements for documentation.

And the most disturbing part—the recognition that actually did penetrate his carefully maintained professional composure—was that he could no longer reliably distinguish between explanations that described what had actually happened and explanations that described what the system needed to have happened.

The gap between those two categories had collapsed.

He was no longer explaining their decisions.

He was explaining the framework's logic using their decisions as examples.

He had become a spokesperson for the system that had broken them.

And he was very, very good at it.

CHAPTER 18

DEMANDS

THE SHIFT DID NOT ANNOUNCE itself through dramatic escalation or explicit threat.

There was no alert tone marking the transition. No escalation marker in the communication headers. No formal notification that the rules had changed.

Just a revision in phrasing so subtle that only someone watching for it would notice.

Mara noticed because she was watching for it.

FOLLOW-UP REQUESTED became **RESPONSE REQUIRED**.

OPTIONAL disappeared from the message classification entirely.

SUGGESTED TIMELINE was replaced by **SCHEDULED SESSION**.

The system no longer suggested cooperation.

It scheduled compliance.

The new summons arrived simultaneously to all five crew members—not staggered across cycles, not allowing for individual preparation or coordination. One transmission. One timestamp. One non-negotiable requirement.

CONSOLIDATION SESSION SCHEDULED

DATE: CURRENT CYCLE + 6 HOURS

ATTENDANCE: MANDATORY FOR ALL CREW

FORMAT: COLLECTIVE RESPONSE VERIFICATION

They were being summoned to the same physical space in the surface habitat—not separate interview rooms allowing individual testimony, not asynchronous text responses that could be carefully composed and edited. One room. One interface. One shared real-time clock that would document exactly who said what and when and how long they hesitated before speaking.

Hale arrived first, precisely at the scheduled time. Then Rourke, thirty seconds later. Then Chen, moving with the deliberate pace of someone consciously controlling visible anxiety. Okoye came last, her medical responsibilities providing legitimate excuse for the brief delay.

Mara stood near the rear wall of the small conference space, her tablet screen dark, present as observer rather than participant. Her role wasn't to answer questions—it was to document how answers were given, to preserve the metadata that would reveal what the official transcript concealed.

No one sat despite chairs being available.

Standing suggested readiness to leave, unwillingness to settle into the process, resistance maintained through posture even when verbal resistance had been abandoned.

The interface activated without preamble or greeting, text appearing on the wall-mounted display:

CONSOLIDATION SESSION: ROUND TWO

PURPOSE: RESOLVE REMAINING DISCREPANCIES IN CREW TESTIMONY

PROTOCOL: COLLECTIVE VERIFICATION OF KEY DECISION POINTS

It addressed them as a group rather than as individuals, converting five separate perspectives into a single collective entity that could be held accountable as a unit.

The first prompt appeared:

Please confirm: activation of the Modified Care Protocol occurred following achievement of group consensus as defined by mission framework requirements.

Silence filled the space between the question's appearance and the expected response.

"Yes," Hale said—too quickly, the word emerging before anyone else had time to formulate their own answer, before the silence could extend long enough to suggest uncertainty or internal disagreement.

CONFIRMATION RECEIVED.

RESPONSE LOGGED: COMMANDER HALE

Mara felt the dynamic shift in that moment. The answer had not been negotiated among the crew before being offered. It had been supplied by the person with institutional authority to speak for the group, and the system had accepted that authority without requiring corroboration from others.

The next prompt appeared immediately:

Please confirm whether any individual objection or reservation altered the final implementation outcome.

Hale started to speak, then stopped—catching himself, perhaps recognizing that answering every question personally would make the "collective" framing obviously false.

"No," Rourke said instead, his voice steady, almost casual in its certainty. "The outcome didn't change regardless of concerns raised during deliberation."

CONFIRMED.

RESPONSE LOGGED: CREW MEMBER ROURKE

Chen inhaled deliberately before speaking, the breath audible over the room's ambient systems noise.

"Objections were voiced during the decision process," he said with careful precision. "They were acknowledged and considered within the framework's evaluation criteria."

He stopped there. Did not elaborate on whether acknowledgment constituted meaningful engagement. Did not specify what "considered" actually meant in practice.

The system waited for continuation.

No one stepped in to complicate the record with additional detail or clarification. The silence that followed Chen's statement was acceptance rather than disagreement.

The third prompt arrived:

Please confirm whether the decision environment could be accurately described as coercive, either through explicit pressure or implicit threat to mission continuation or crew safety.

"No," Rourke said immediately, the response automatic.

"No," Hale echoed half a second later, his affirmation slower but equally definitive.

Chen did not speak.

Okoye did not speak.

Their silence registered differently than active denial—not quite agreement, but not quite objection either. Passive acceptance of what others had already confirmed.

ALIGNMENT IMPROVING.

RESPONSE CONVERGENCE: 87%

The system was quantifying their consensus in real-time, measuring linguistic variance and temporal patterns, calculating how closely their individual statements aligned with the desired collective narrative.

Mara watched the metadata display at the bottom of the screen—response length compressing toward brevity, hesitation intervals shortening, variance decreasing across successive prompts. They were learning what the room rewarded. Simple affirmation over complex explanation. Agreement over qualification. Closure over continued deliberation.

A final prompt resolved on screen:

For final record clarity: please confirm that medical objections were formally noted during deliberation but were ultimately overridden by collective decision to prioritize mission continuity.

No name was attached to the question. No designated speaker assigned. The absence of specificity was itself significant—the system was allowing them to choose who would voice this particular confirmation, who would explicitly acknowledge that objection had been subordinated to institutional necessity.

Chen looked at Okoye. Just for a moment. A glance that might have been asking permission, or offering support, or simply acknowledging that this statement belonged to her more than to anyone else.

"Yes," Okoye said, her voice quiet but clear. "My medical objections were noted in the decision record and were subsequently overridden by consensus prioritization of mission survival."

ACKNOWLEDGED.

RESPONSE LOGGED: MEDICAL OFFICER OKOYE

Then, after a calculated pause:

RESPONSE CONVERGENCE ACHIEVED: 94%

NARRATIVE ALIGNMENT: ACCEPTABLE

NO FURTHER CLARIFICATION REQUIRED AT THIS TIME

The interface went dark.

The session had concluded.

They stood there together in the suddenly silent space, five people arranged in loose formation, carefully not looking at one another directly, not making eye contact that might reveal what they were thinking, what they actually felt about what they'd just collectively validated.

The system had not forced the answers through explicit coercion or threat of punishment.

They had supplied them voluntarily, following the pathways the questions had constructed, accepting the framing the prompts had offered, using the language the framework had provided.

That evening, they gathered for the communal meal period as usual.

No one avoided the galley table. No one rushed through eating to minimize shared time. But no one initiated conversation either. No one offered observations about the day's work or commented on the consolidation session they'd all just participated in.

Small talk had become evidence. Casual conversation was potential testimony. Any statement could be archived and analyzed and used to identify inconsistencies with official positions.

Silence was safer.

Okoye finished eating last. She stood, collected her tray, moved it to the cleaning station. Then paused, standing at the edge of the communal space, looking at the others without quite meeting anyone's eyes.

"They got what they wanted," she said quietly. Not quite accusation, not quite resignation. Just recognition of outcome.

No one disagreed.

No one affirmed either.

The statement hung in the air, neither confirmed nor denied, accurate enough that contradiction was impossible but specific enough that elaboration felt dangerous.

Later, alone in her quarters during the sleep period she was increasingly unable to use for actual rest, Mara did not open the archive of unedited footage she'd been maintaining.

She did not need to review the evidence of what had been erased from the official record.

The system had resolved its discrepancy without requiring that evidence. Had achieved alignment through patient application of pressure disguised as clarification. Had converted resistance into compliance through accumulated small surrenders that added up to complete capitulation.

Alignment had been achieved.

94% convergence. Acceptable narrative coherence. No further clarification required.

And she knew—with the archivist's understanding of how institutions processed difficult history—that explanation never distributed evenly when accountability came due. Someone always carried more weight than others. Someone always became the case study, the cautionary example, the individual whose choices would be examined while collective decisions were abstracted into policy lessons.

The system would eventually decide who that someone was.

Who would be remembered as the objector whose concerns were overridden.

Who would be framed as the dissenter whose resistance proved insufficient.

Who would carry the narrative weight of individual moral failure while collective institutional logic was preserved and propagated.

This time, the system wouldn't need to ask who should bear that burden.

Okoye had just volunteered the answer herself.

My medical objections were noted in the decision record and were subsequently overridden.

The statement was accurate. Documented. Spoken in her own voice, preserved in official records, impossible to later deny or reframe.

And it was exactly what the framework needed to convert collective institutional failure into individual case study.

The archive Mara had been preserving—the unedited footage showing hesitation and doubt and the complexity of impossible choices—might never matter.

The official record was complete without it.

Alignment had been achieved.

CHAPTER 19

OUTCOME

THE FAULT WAS MINOR.

So minor it did not register as an alert in the habitat's automated monitoring systems. No threshold violation. No red indicators. No automated notification demanding immediate attention.

Just a deviation from ideal that remained technically within acceptable operational parameters.

Rourke felt it during routine maintenance inspection—an irregular vibration in the secondary cooling loop, the one buried in the regolith berm that provided thermal stability for the habitat's environmental control systems. Barely outside nominal resonance frequency. The kind of subtle mechanical irregularity he would normally correct immediately, almost reflexively, before it could develop into something more serious.

He stood there longer than the inspection protocol required, one gloved hand resting against the access panel, feeling the tremor transmit through composite material into his palm. A rhythm that wasn't quite right. A vibration that suggested imperfect alignment somewhere in the coolant circulation pathway.

Within tolerance.

The words arrived in his mind unbidden, using language that had become automatic through repetition, through accumulated exposure to frameworks that defined acceptable deviation.

He checked the diagnostic readouts displayed on the panel-mounted interface. Flow rate steady. Temperature differential within expected range. Pressure holding. No alerts. No warnings.

The numbers agreed with his assessment: technically functional, operationally acceptable, not requiring intervention according to system thresholds.

He closed the access panel.

Sealed it carefully. Logged the inspection timestamp.

The vibration continued behind the sealed panel, unchanged by his attention or his decision not to address it.

Rourke logged the maintenance check as complete. No exceptions noted. No action items generated.

Later that same sol, during a geological sampling traverse across the crater floor, Chen mentioned a minor temperature variance he'd noticed near the habitat's aft section during his morning sensor review.

"Probably related to the secondary cooling loop," Rourke said, his tone carefully neutral, neither confirming a problem nor dismissing the observation. "I checked it this morning. Reading shows it's within acceptable range."

Chen nodded, accepting the assessment without pressing for additional detail. "I'll flag it for continued monitoring in case the trend develops."

Neither of them moved to actually fix the underlying issue.

Neither of them suggested that "within acceptable range" might not be the same as "optimal" or "should be addressed proactively."

The cooling loop vibrated through the night cycle—not loudly enough to penetrate into the sleeping quarters, not dramatically enough to wake anyone who wasn't already listening for it specifically.

But audible if you knew where to place your attention. Persistent if you allowed yourself to notice.

Rourke woke before the scheduled alarms as he always did, his internal clock precisely calibrated despite Martian sol length. He lay still in his bunk, listening to the habitat's ambient sounds.

The vibration was there. Unchanged. Steady in its irregularity.

He could fix it. The repair would be straightforward—access the loop at the maintenance junction, identify the source of the resonance, adjust the mounting brackets or replace a worn bearing or recalibrate the pump motor. An hour of work, maybe two. Well within his technical capability. Exactly the kind of preventive maintenance that his training had emphasized, that his professional identity was built around performing.

He did not get up.

Did not initiate the repair sequence.

Did not add the task to his personal work queue.

The next day he recalibrated a different system instead—one that was already performing optimally, that showed no deviation from specifications. The thermal regulation for the greenhouse module that they'd suspended lighting to during the dust storm. He adjusted control parameters. Verified the adjustments. Logged the work. Then adjusted them again slightly, confirming that the system responded correctly to input changes.

Precision still mattered to him.

Just not everywhere. Not uniformly. Not without discrimination about which systems warranted intervention and which could be allowed to persist in suboptimal states as long as they remained within defined tolerances.

Mara observed the oscillation in background telemetry data while reviewing daily system logs. Small compensatory adjustments propagating through related subsystems. Power draw redistributing slightly between the reactor baseline and solar array contribution. Battery cycling patterns shifting by fractions of a percent to balance load more evenly.

The habitat's automated control systems were adapting quietly to the cooling loop's degraded performance, making micro-corrections that maintained overall stability despite the local fault.

She did not log the observation as requiring attention. There was no formal reason to do so. No alert had fired. No threshold had been violated. The system was compensating successfully.

Hale reviewed the daily mission summary report before authorizing its transmission to Earth.

All systems nominal.

No maintenance exceptions requiring documentation.

No action items pending escalation.

Surface operations proceeding within planned parameters.

He approved the summary without modification or added commentary.

The report transmitted during the next scheduled communications window, adding another data point to the accumulated evidence that the mission was functioning exactly as designed, that all challenges were being managed within established frameworks.

Okoye passed through the engineering section during a routine transit between habitat levels. Felt the vibration through the deck plating beneath her boots. A subtle wrongness in the mechanical ambience that her medical training made her sensitive to—the way a physician learns to notice asymmetries and irregularities that others might dismiss as normal variation.

She paused. Placed her hand against the bulkhead. Felt the tremor clearly.

"Is something off with the environmental systems?" she asked Rourke, who was nearby reviewing power distribution displays.

Rourke didn't look up from his interface. "No."

Single word. Definitive. Allowing no space for further inquiry.

She waited half a beat, hand still against the vibrating bulkhead, considering whether to press the question or accept the answer.

She moved on.

By the third cycle after initial detection, the compensation patterns had stabilized. The habitat's systems had found their new equilibrium around the cooling loop's degraded performance. Power distribution held steady despite slightly increased load on supplementary systems. Thermal regulation maintained target temperatures through increased reactor contribution.

Efficiency metrics showed minor reduction—fractions of a percent, well within mission planning margins.

No alert ever fired.

The loop remained unfixed.

Rourke stood alone in the engineering bay during his off-shift hours, ostensibly performing routine inspections but actually just listening to the habitat hum around the flaw it had successfully absorbed into normal operation.

He knew exactly where the problem was located. Could visualize the specific component that was generating the irregular vibration. Could estimate the repair duration with professional accuracy.

He also knew that the problem was stable. Not worsening. Not threatening to cascade into larger failure. Just persisting at a constant level of degradation that the system had learned to accommodate.

Within tolerance.

The framework that had once described acceptable deviation had become permission to ignore.

He pulled up the maintenance log on his tablet. Found the entry from his inspection three sols previous.

Added a new line:

Follow-up check performed. Status unchanged. Continued monitoring recommended.

Logged it as complete.

Closed the interface.

The vibration continued its steady rhythm, a flaw woven into the habitat's normal function, persistent and ignored, maintained rather than repaired.

Just like Jonah in orbit.

Just like everything they'd learned to accept as inevitable when the alternative required resources they'd already allocated elsewhere, energy they'd already expended, attention they'd already redirected toward priorities the framework had defined as more important.

Rourke stood in the engineering bay, surrounded by systems that mostly worked, listening to the one that didn't quite work but worked well enough.

Precision still mattered.

He still believed that.

But precision had learned to coexist with acceptable tolerance for imperfection.

And he had learned not to fix everything that could be fixed.

Only the things that had to be fixed.

Only the failures that couldn't be absorbed.

The distinction had once been clear to him—technical judgment about when intervention was necessary versus when it was optional.

Now the distinction felt arbitrary. Convenient. A rationalization for passivity disguised as professional assessment.

He left the engineering bay without addressing the cooling loop.

Logged his inspection as complete.

All systems nominal.

The language held.

Even when the reality it described was something else entirely.

CHAPTER 20
RETURN

THE RETURN from Mars surface began exactly twenty-one days after landing, the timing dictated by orbital mechanics rather than readiness or preference, by the immutable mathematics of planetary positions and fuel reserves and transfer windows that existed independent of human desire.

The DAV rested on Jezero regolith where it had touched down three weeks prior, landing struts compressed under Martian gravity—0.38 Earth g, enough to hold things down but not enough to feel entirely real. Fuel reserves had been calculated to the gram during mission planning, margins verified and reverified until no uncertainty remained. Ascent window: four hours from current position. Margin for delay: none.

The physics dictated departure. They complied.

They suited up in silence, backing through their designated suitports one final time, sealing themselves into the EVA suits that had remained mounted on the DAV's exterior throughout the surface mission, dust-coated and radiation-exposed but still functional within specifications.

Okoye was last to board the DAV's crew compartment. She paused at the hatch, one boot on the ladder, one still on Martian ground—the last moment of direct physical contact with the surface they'd traveled millions of kilometers to reach.

She looked back once. At the surface habitat that would remain buried under its protective berms, systems powered down to minimum, waiting for a future mission that might never come. At the equipment they were leaving behind—rovers, sensor arrays, sample containers, infrastructure that represented years of planning and billions in resources. At the red plain stretching toward a horizon that remained too close despite three weeks of acclimation, Mars' smaller radius making distant things feel nearer than they should.

They had been here.

That would have to be enough.

"Hatch sealed," Rourke confirmed from inside, his voice compressed through the comm system.

"Confirmed," Hale replied, running through the pre-launch checklist with methodical precision. "CONCORDIA, this is DAV-1. Initiating pre-launch sequence. Request status confirmation."

A pause—communication lag climbing from surface to orbit, nine-tenths of a second each direction, enough delay to make conversation feel disconnected.

Then Jonah's voice: "Copy, DAV-1. Standing by for ascent. All orbital systems green. Ready for rendezvous procedures."

Still steady. Still professional. Still alone after three weeks of solitary orbital watch.

"How's orbital status?" Hale asked, the question casual but carrying weight neither of them acknowledged.

"Nominal. All systems within acceptable parameters. CONCORDIA is ready for crew transfer and Earth departure burn."

Three weeks.

Jonah had been alone aboard CONCORDIA for three weeks—maintaining systems, monitoring telemetry, performing the orbital watch duties they'd assigned him when the Modified Care Protocol made surface operations impossible, when his conversion into infrastructure had been formalized and documented and accepted as necessary.

The DAV's ascent engine ignited with violence that felt personal rather than mechanical. Chemical fury translated into acceleration. Mars fell away beneath them with disturbing speed—red plain flattening into abstraction, then curving at the edges, then disappearing entirely as they climbed into the black.

The g-forces pressed them into their seats with pressure that made breathing deliberate. Chen's respiration quickened audibly over the comm channel, stress response to acceleration that training couldn't entirely eliminate. Rourke monitored structural stress indicators without speaking, watching numbers that confirmed the vehicle was holding together despite forces trying to tear it apart.

Okoye closed her eyes against the acceleration, against the view through the small viewport, against everything except the simple fact of motion—leaving the surface, ascending to orbit, returning to CONCORDIA.

To Jonah.

The ascent profile was clean, textbook perfect. Trajectory nominal. Fuel expenditure tracking within two percent of projections. All systems performing exactly as designed.

"CONCORDIA, we're showing orbital insertion in ninety seconds," Hale reported as the ascent engine cut off and they transitioned to maneuvering thrusters.

"Copy, DAV-1. I have you on approach radar. Docking alignment confirmed. Closing velocity within parameters."

The DAV's reaction control thrusters fired in brief, precise bursts—tiny corrections to velocity and orientation, refining their approach vector. CONCORDIA grew in the viewport from distant point to recognizable structure, angular and geometric and familiar.

Home. The only structure in millions of kilometers that knew all six of them, that contained the accumulated context of their journey.

"Twenty meters," Jonah reported, his voice steady despite three weeks of isolation, despite whatever the protocol had done to him during that time. "Relative velocity good. Alignment nominal. You're cleared for final approach."

"Confirmed," Hale replied.

"Ten meters."

The docking collar loomed in the viewport. Mara watched it approach with the slow inevitability of orbital mechanics—velocities measured in centimeters per second, closing distance with patience that felt almost geological.

"Contact in three, two, one..."

A soft thud transmitted through the DAV's hull. Mechanical engagement. Clamps engaging with precise timing. Seals verifying pressure integrity.

"Docking complete," Jonah said. "Initiating tunnel pressurization. Stand by for hatch clearance."

They waited, hearts still racing from ascent g-forces, suits still sealed, breathing recycled air that tasted of exertion and stress and the peculiar staleness of oxygen that had cycled through too many bodies.

Pressure equalized between DAV and CONCORDIA. Green indicators lit sequentially across the status panel as automated systems confirmed seal integrity, atmospheric composition, structural connection.

"You're clear to open," Jonah said.

Hale unsealed the hatch manually, rotating the mechanical locks that separated pressurized environments, the final physical barrier between them and reunion.

It opened into CONCORDIA's docking bay—familiar geometry that their bodies recognized before their minds processed, the enclosing structure that had been their entire world for months before Mars, that would be their world again for months until Earth.

The only environment that still knew all of them.

Jonah stood just inside the docking bay, positioned near the hatch to receive them.

Not suited for EVA. Not strapped into restraints. Standing upright under the gentle pull of CONCORDIA's slow rotation creating artificial gravity. Hands loose at his sides rather than braced against surfaces.

But changed.

Visibly changed.

Thinner—not dramatically, but noticeably. Hollowed slightly at the cheeks, the facial structure more prominent than it had been before surface operations. His eyes tracked them as they emerged from the DAV one by one, still wearing their helmets, still transitioning between environments.

Aware. Present. Functioning.

"Welcome back," he said.

His voice had not changed. Still carried the same tone, the same inflection patterns. The Modified Care Protocol had maintained his vocal capability even as it had adjusted everything else.

But his status—the category he occupied, the role he performed, the relationship he had to the mission and to them—that had changed fundamentally and irrevocably.

Okoye removed her helmet first, breaking the seal with practiced efficiency. The air inside CONCORDIA tasted recycled and stale—exactly as it had before they'd departed for the surface, unchanged by three weeks of time, preserved by systems that didn't distinguish between inhabited and abandoned spaces.

"How are you?" she asked. The question direct, unambiguous, asking about him rather than about system status.

"Operational," Jonah replied, defaulting to the language the protocol had made automatic. "All systems maintained during surface operations. No critical alerts logged. CONCORDIA is ready for Earth return trajectory."

"That's not what I asked."

He smiled. The expression formed correctly—lips curving, facial muscles engaging appropriately. But it didn't reach his eyes, didn't carry genuine warmth or connection. Mechanical rather than emotional.

"I know," he said.

For a moment—just one, suspended between acknowledgment and response—no one moved. Five people fresh from Mars surface, one person who'd remained in orbit, all of them trapped in the gap between what they could say and what they actually meant.

Then Rourke stepped forward abruptly and pulled Jonah into an embrace. Brief. Hard. Physical contact that conveyed what language couldn't.

When he pulled back, his eyes were wet. Tears floating in microgravity before being absorbed by air circulation.

"I'm glad you're okay," Rourke said, voice rough with emotion he hadn't permitted himself to express during the surface mission.

"I did my job," Jonah replied. Not deflecting, just stating fact. "Maintained the ship. Monitored systems. Provided orbital support. That's what the protocol assigned."

Chen nodded, unable to speak, throat closed against words that wouldn't come.

Mara recorded none of it. Her camera remained stowed, the moment too private for documentation, too raw for the archive that would eventually be studied and analyzed and converted into lessons learned.

Hale placed a hand on Jonah's shoulder—steady, paternal, the gesture exactly like the one captured in their pre-mission training photograph when they'd still been six people preparing for shared adventure rather than five people and one who'd been optimized into infrastructure.

"Good work," he said. Commander's approval. Official recognition of duty performed.

Jonah stood very still under the contact.

"Thank you, Commander."

Okoye looked at him and felt something collapse inside her chest—not quite grief, not quite guilt, something that encompassed both but exceeded either. An emotion she had no clean name for.

They had left him in orbit.

They had descended to Mars while he remained aboard CONCORDIA, alone, maintained by protocols and pharmaceuticals and automated systems.

They had walked on another planet. Had collected samples. Had conducted experiments. Had made history.

Jonah had stayed aboard CONCORDIA, maintaining systems that kept them alive, monitoring telemetry that ensured their safe return, performing orbital watch duties that made their achievement possible.

The protocol had preserved them all.

That was the promise the framework had made.

That was the lie they'd accepted.

The return to Earth began without ceremony or formal acknowledgment.

No countdown marking transition. No applause celebrating departure. Just automated checks clearing one by one, systems confirming readiness, CONCORDIA's engines firing according to pre-programmed sequences.

The mothership eased free of Mars orbit as if leaving a room it had never truly entered, departing with the same mechanical indifference it had arrived with.

Mars receded in the viewports—red disk, then point, then nothing distinguishable from the black. The planet that had justified everything disappeared without acknowledgment.

No one marked the moment.

No one stood at the observation ports watching their departure.

No one suggested they should pause to recognize what they were leaving behind.

Hale moved through the departure sequence with practiced ease, procedure returning to him like native language after the improvised challenges of surface operations. Commands issued. Confirmations received. Systems responding exactly as designed.

"Departure burn nominal," he reported.

"Confirmed," Chen replied from his station. "Trajectory aligns with Earth return corridor."

"Thermal management holding," Rourke added. "All cooling systems within operating parameters."

Okoye monitored Jonah's medical status without comment, watching indicators that confirmed what she already knew.

Stable.

The word that meant everything and nothing.

Mid-cycle during the first day of return transit, a minor system variance surfaced—thermal drift along a secondary coolant conduit, the same fault that had started on the surface and had never been properly addressed.

Non-critical. Trending slowly but contained within tolerance. Predictable rather than alarming.

"Assessment," Hale requested, not specifying who should respond but expecting someone to.

Chen answered immediately, numbers already calculated. "Within tolerance. Predictable degradation slope. No intervention threshold crossed."

Rourke followed without hesitation, solution already formulated. "Bypass reroute will redistribute thermal load. No long-term mission penalty."

Hale nodded acceptance. "Proceed with reroute."

No discussion. No debate. No second evaluation or alternative perspectives.

They executed the correction efficiently. The thermal alert cleared. Systems stabilized.

It was the cleanest technical decision they'd made since Mars orbit insertion.

No one smiled at the efficiency.

No one acknowledged how easily they'd converged on solution without disagreement or uncertainty.

They simply dispersed back into individual routines as if nothing significant had happened, as if competence restored was somehow normal rather than notable.

Okoye sat beside Jonah in the medical bay without speaking, monitoring systems that confirmed his continued stability while offering no path toward recovery.

Chen closed his workstation terminal earlier than his usual schedule dictated, fatigue overriding discipline.

Rourke washed his hands once after maintenance work and stopped, resisting the compulsion to repeat the action that had become ritual during surface operations.

Hale reviewed the Earth return trajectory one final time, verified all parameters, then approved it without adding notes or qualifications.

The return proceeded exactly as planned.

Technical competence had returned—the crew's ability to function as trained operators of complex systems, to make decisions efficiently, to execute procedures without friction or doubt.

Meaning had not.

They had all made it to Mars.

But only five had touched it.

Only five had stood on the surface and felt alien gravity and looked at distant horizons.

And that difference—small in practical terms, procedural in justification, rational within the framework that had defined it—would follow them home.

Would persist in the space between them.

Would become part of the permanent record that documented their achievement while erasing what that achievement had cost.

CHAPTER 21
CONTACT

CONTACT WITH EARTH'S atmosphere began as pressure.

Not the gentle reminder of gravity gradually increasing during orbital descent, but sudden physical force—CONCORDIA shuddering violently as it encountered air molecules after months in vacuum, the transition from frictionless space to viscous atmosphere marked by heat and noise and vibration that felt personal rather than mechanical.

Systems compensated automatically for forces that would have torn the ship apart without careful engineering. Heat shields ablating in controlled fashion, converting kinetic energy to thermal energy and dispersing it away from the crew compartment. Drag building exponentially as they descended into denser atmosphere. Trajectory tightening in real time as guidance systems made continuous micro-adjustments to keep them within the narrow corridor between burning up and skipping back into space.

Mara felt the deceleration in her teeth—jaw clenched against g-forces, the vibration transmitting through her skull, through bone rather than flesh.

Hale called checkpoints by reflex, commander's voice steady despite the chaos. "Heat shield temp nominal. Trajectory within corridor. Velocity decreasing as projected."

Chen confirmed readings from his station, hands moving across interfaces with practiced precision even as acceleration pressed him into his restraints. "Confirmed. All parameters green. Descent profile nominal."

Rourke monitored structural integrity displays, watching stress indicators that showed exactly how close they were to the vehicle's design limits. "Hull stress acceptable. No breach warnings. Structure holding."

Okoye stayed in the medical bay despite protocol recommendations that all crew be in primary couches for entry. One hand braced against Jonah's medical pod, the other steadying herself against bulkheads as CONCORDIA bucked and twisted through atmospheric turbulence.

For several minutes during the peak deceleration phase, their bodies remembered coordination without requiring conscious deliberation or verbal agreement. Trained responses executing automatically. Crew functioning as designed despite everything that had fractured between them.

Then the drogue parachutes deployed with violent deceleration. Drag bit hard, sudden and massive. Earth's gravity returned in increments that felt personal after months in microgravity—not the abstract force of orbital mechanics but weight pressing down on chest and limbs, making breathing require deliberate effort.

"Main chutes deployed," Hale reported. "Descent nominal."

Nominal.

The word that had followed them from Earth to Mars and back again. The word that meant everything was functioning within acceptable parameters even when nothing felt acceptable.

They landed in ocean rather than desert, splashdown occurring exactly within the projected landing zone despite winds and currents and the accumulated uncertainties of atmospheric entry.

The impact was gentler than Mara expected—an abrupt stop as CONCORDIA hit water, then immediate transition to the slow rocking motion of being carried by waves rather than carrying oneself through space. Floating rather than flying. Supported rather than autonomous.

Ocean.

Liquid water in vast quantities. Salt spray visible through the viewport. The particular blue-green of Earth's seas that no other planet replicated.

For a moment after splashdown, no one spoke. The silence filled with the sound of waves slapping against CONCORDIA's hull, of recovery systems activating, of home arriving without announcement or ceremony.

Then the communication channel opened—ground control reestablishing contact after entry blackout, human voices replacing the isolation of descent.

A voice from Earth arrived warm, inflected with genuine emotion rather than the professional neutrality that had characterized mission communications. Human in a way no protocol could successfully imitate, no framework could adequately replicate.

"CONCORDIA, welcome home," it said. "You did it. First humans to Mars and back. You actually did it."

Applause filtered through the channel—delayed slightly by radio transmission, distorted by compression and distance, but unmistakably celebratory. Cheering. Shouting. Joy expressed without institutional constraint.

Mara watched the others respond to the sound.

Rourke closed his eyes, jaw tightening, fighting visible emotion.

Chen stared at the deck plating between his feet, unable or unwilling to acknowledge the celebration.

Okoye pressed her palm flat against Jonah's medical pod—contact with the person who couldn't participate in this moment, who was present but absent, alive but not quite living.

Hale nodded once, accepting the recognition like a duty he was obligated to receive rather than an achievement he could celebrate.

"Thank you, Ground Control," he said, voice steady and professional. "We're glad to be back."

Recovery teams boarded quickly—the hatch opening to admit personnel in flotation gear, hands reaching to assist, voices overlapping with instructions and congratulations. Equipment flooding the capsule's confined space. The sudden presence of other humans after months of isolation, of faces that didn't belong to the crew, of people who hadn't shared the journey.

The hatch opened to daylight so bright it physically hurt after months of artificial illumination and the black of space. Natural sunlight unfiltered by viewport glass. Earth's atmosphere scattering wavelengths into blue sky.

Earth smelled wet and alive—salt water and organic decomposition and atmospheric moisture, complex chemistry that spacecraft air recycling could never replicate.

Jonah was transferred last, after the ambulatory crew had already been assisted from their couches and guided toward the recovery vessel.

Okoye followed automatically, medical authority settling into her voice without conscious effort. "I'm primary physician on his care. I need to accompany during transfer."

"You did great, Doctor," someone said gently—a recovery medic, professional and kind but firm. "We'll take it from here. Our team is fully briefed on his condition. You've done everything you could."

They moved between her and the medical pod. Not abruptly or aggressively. Not unkindly.

Just—present. Numerous. Institutional rather than individual.

She stepped back, allowing the separation, watching as they carefully extracted Jonah's pod from CONCORDIA's medical bay and began the transfer to the recovery vessel's equipped medical facility.

Separation followed almost immediately after extraction from the capsule. Medical checks conducted in separate facilities. Decontamination procedures performed individually. Health assessments administered with smooth efficiency by personnel who'd been preparing for this moment while the crew was still in transit.

Process reclaimed them, dividing six into individuals again, converting the collective experience back into separate data points that could be evaluated and categorized and documented according to institutional requirements.

The first camera appeared sooner than Mara expected—not press cameras, not celebration documentation.

An institutional lens. Matte-black casing. The same model she recognized from mission control recordings. Familiar equipment operated by familiar processes.

"Just a preliminary statement," the camera operator explained, positioning equipment with professional efficiency. "For mission continuity. We'll do a full debrief later, but we need something immediate for the record."

Continuity.

The word suggested connection, narrative flow, maintained coherence between departure and return.

Mara smiled because continuity required it, because maintaining the expected response was automatic after months of performing for cameras, for archives, for the record that would outlive them all.

Hale delivered the first official statement on solid ground—standing on the recovery vessel's deck, Earth's ocean visible behind him, his words measured and calm and appropriately grateful.

"This mission represents the best of human capability," he said, using phrasing that had been workshopped during training, refined through repetition, optimized for institutional consumption. "We're honored to have carried this responsibility on behalf of everyone who made it possible."

Then, because the script required it, because the moment had been planned years in advance:

"For all mankind," he said again.

The phrase that had marked their departure. That had accompanied their landing on Mars. That now closed the circle of their journey.

The recovery personnel nodded. Some applauded. The camera recorded.

The story took hold—the narrative that would be propagated through media channels, analyzed in academic papers, taught in schools, preserved in archives as the official account of the first human mission to Mars.

Later, in temporary quarters at the recovery facility—individual rooms rather than shared habitat, privacy restored after months of forced proximity—Mara's personal tablet chimed with a notification.

ARCHIVE STATUS: INTACT

FILE INTEGRITY: VERIFIED

UNAUTHORIZED ACCESS: NONE DETECTED

She stared at the screen for several minutes, processing implications.

The archive she'd maintained separately from official channels—the unedited footage showing hesitation and doubt, the timestamps revealing editing, the evidence of what had been optimized out of the institutional record—remained secure.

No one had accessed it. No one had deleted it. No one had even attempted to discover its existence.

Which meant either her security was adequate...

Or the institutional record was already complete enough that contradictory evidence didn't matter, that alternative narratives were irrelevant when the official version had achieved sufficient coherence and distribution.

Mara closed the display without making any immediate decision about what to do with the archive.

Contact wasn't a moment, she realized.

It was a process.

A gradual reintegration into institutional structures. A careful reconciliation of individual experience with collective narrative. A patient alignment of what had happened with what needed to be remembered.

They had returned to Earth.

But Earth had its own frameworks waiting to receive them.

Its own protocols for processing what they'd done.

Its own language for describing achievement and sacrifice and the price of historic accomplishment.

And those frameworks—patient, comprehensive, designed by people who understood how stories needed to be told—would shape what their mission meant regardless of what they'd actually experienced.

The record would be preserved.

But preservation wasn't the same as truth.

She knew that better than anyone.

CHAPTER 22
LEVERAGE

THE FIRST REQUEST arrived wrapped in courtesy, bureaucratic politeness disguising institutional compulsion.

REQUEST: AVAILABILITY FOR FOLLOW-UP DISCUSSION

PURPOSE: CONTEXTUAL CONTINUITY

FORMAT: OFF-RECORD

Off-record meant: we won't quote you unless we need to. We won't hold you accountable for what you say unless it becomes convenient. We're offering you the illusion of privacy so you'll speak more freely, and then we'll use what you say however serves institutional purposes.

They were housed separately now—individual rooms in the recovery facility rather than shared crew quarters, the physical separation justified through logistics but functioning as isolation. Individual schedules preventing casual coordination. Staggered debrief windows ensuring no two crew members were ever processed simultaneously. Privacy framed as recovery consideration, separation presented as care rather than control.

Mara noticed the pattern immediately because recognizing patterns was her professional expertise, the archivist's trained attention to how information was structured and managed.

Isolate inputs.

Process individually.

Reconcile outputs afterward.

The classic methodology for extracting consistent testimony—prevent subjects from coordinating stories, interview them separately, identify discrepancies, apply pressure at the weak points until alignment is achieved.

Chen received his invitation framed as praise disguised as request: *We'd love to have you walk our engineering review committee through your methodology. Your approach to resource optimization was exemplary. Would you be available for a brief technical consultation?*

Rourke received a calendar notification with no subject line, just a time block marked **REQUIRED ATTENDANCE** and a room number.

Okoye was summoned for wellness screening—psychological evaluation presented as standard medical procedure, the kind of health monitoring that was supposedly routine but that never quite asked directly how she actually felt about what they'd done.

Hale accepted the off-record consultation without consulting the other crew members first. He told himself that maintaining control of the narrative was protection—that if he managed the institutional interface carefully enough, he could shield the others from scrutiny, could contain the damage, could ensure the right story emerged from review.

He told himself this was leadership rather than complicity.

The liaison appeared on his video screen precisely at the scheduled time —professionally neutral expression, concern carefully calibrated to suggest empathy without actually offering anything, tone modulated to sound supportive while extracting information.

"Commander Hale, congratulations on an extraordinary achievement," she began, establishing rapport through recognition. "What you accomplished is already shaping doctrine for future deep space missions. The framework you operated within is being studied intensively."

Doctrine.

Not history. Not achievement. Doctrine—the institutionalized lessons that would be extracted from their experience and propagated as binding guidance for others.

"I understand there are some questions about implementation details," Hale said, maintaining professional composure while acknowledging the real purpose of this consultation.

"Clarifications," the liaison corrected gently, reframing interrogation as collaborative refinement. "Our goal is alignment with established protocols, not fault-finding. We're simply ensuring that the documented record accurately reflects the decision-making process you employed."

Alignment.

The word that had followed them from Mars orbit through surface operations through return journey. Always alignment. Never truth. Never accuracy independent of institutional requirements.

She asked about decision thresholds—when had they determined that Modified Care was necessary rather than optional?

He answered with the timeline they'd already documented, the sequence of events that had been logged and transmitted and reviewed.

She asked about timeline compression—had there been sufficient deliberation time, or had urgency created pressure that compromised thoughtful evaluation?

He answered that while circumstances were urgent, the framework had provided adequate structure for making necessary decisions under constraint.

She asked about dissent—had there been disagreement, and if so, how had it been addressed?

"There were differing perspectives," Hale said, using language he'd refined through multiple previous iterations of this explanation. "Which is expected under high-stress conditions. Different professional backgrounds, different risk assessments, different priorities."

"And how were those differences resolved?"

"Through consensus," Hale said. "Through discussion and deliberation until we reached collective agreement on the necessary course of action."

The word came easily now. Automatically. Without requiring conscious consideration of whether it accurately described what had actually happened or simply described what the framework required to have happened.

"Good," the liaison said, tone carrying subtle approval. "That matches the record we've compiled from other sources."

Matches.

Not *is*. Not *confirms* or *verifies*.

Matches—suggesting comparison with a standard that existed independent of his testimony, that his words were being evaluated against rather than incorporated into.

Mara's consultation arrived later that same day—no video interface this time, just a shared data screen and a voice tuned to perfect neutrality, gender-ambiguous and professionally modulated.

They asked about her archival procedures. About redundancy protocols. About integrity verification systems. About failure mode analysis and backup procedures.

She answered cleanly, precisely, providing technical details about data management without revealing anything about what she'd actually preserved or why.

Then, almost casually, as if it were merely another routine technical question:

"And of course, any unofficial archival material you may have maintained would follow the same encryption and retention standards as official documentation, yes?"

Fishing.

Not asking if such material existed—assuming it did, inviting her to discuss it as if its existence were already established fact.

"Any archive I maintain," Mara said carefully, choosing words with deliberate precision, "follows appropriate security protocols. Official or otherwise."

A pause. Brief. Measured.

"Consistency simplifies review processes," the voice replied. Not quite threat, not quite advice. Just observation about how institutional systems functioned more smoothly when data aligned properly, when contradictions didn't require resolution.

That night, alone in her assigned quarters, Mara checked the archive status again—not out of habit or routine maintenance, but from calculated concern about what the consultation had implied.

The access logs displayed clean and unremarkable until the final entry.

A system sweep. Read-only access. No user credentials attached to the log entry.

Automated, supposedly. Routine maintenance scanning, theoretically.

But the timestamp coincided precisely with the period when oversight inquiries had been most active. And the scan pattern was nested just far enough upstream in the system architecture to register as background maintenance rather than targeted review.

No file had been opened. No content had been accessed. No alert had been triggered.

But something had looked.

Had identified the archive's existence. Had catalogued its location. Had noted its presence for potential future action.

Mara sat with the screen dimmed, hands motionless on the desk surface, processing implications.

The archive had not been touched—but it had been noticed.

For the first time since she'd created the parallel record, the risk ran both directions.

Keeping the file no longer protected her from institutional narrative control.

It exposed her to institutional scrutiny as someone maintaining contradictory documentation, as someone who might present problems for alignment efforts.

Elsewhere in the recovery facility, individual interviews proceeded according to schedule.

Rourke's meeting concluded in exactly twelve minutes. The interviewer thanked him for his candor, for his straightforward responses, for his cooperative attitude.

"During the decision process," the interviewer had asked, "did anyone formally object to the Modified Care Protocol activation?"

Rourke had shrugged—casual gesture suggesting the question's irrelevance. "Not that I recall. Everyone understood what the situation required."

Not quite lie. Not quite truth. Just selective memory shaped by months of performing alignment, of learning what the framework rewarded.

Chen's session lasted longer—forty-three minutes of walking through resource calculations, of explaining mathematical models, of demonstrating how the numbers had dictated their choice.

"Would you adjust your approach if faced with similar circumstances in the future?" someone asked near the session's conclusion.

"Yes," Chen said without hesitation.

"How specifically?"

He paused, considering. Then answered with the optimization the framework wanted to hear: "I'd define thresholds earlier in the mission planning phase. Establish clear activation criteria before crisis conditions develop."

The answer satisfied them. The pen stopped moving. The interview concluded.

Perfect institutional response—accepting the framework's logic, proposing procedural improvements rather than questioning fundamental assumptions, converting tragedy into lesson learned.

Okoye's evaluation was framed as wellness care rather than interrogation.

"How are you sleeping?" the evaluator asked, clipboard ready to document responses that would be categorized and analyzed.

"I'm functional," Okoye said, defaulting to the language that had become automatic.

"And emotionally? How are you processing the experience?"

Okoye met the evaluator's eyes directly. "I'm compliant."

The pen hesitated mid-notation. The evaluator looked up, expression shifting toward concern or confusion.

"That wasn't the question I asked, Doctor."

"I know," Okoye said.

The response hung in the air—not quite refusal to answer, not quite answer to a different question. Just recognition that the gap between what was being asked and what could be truthfully stated had become unbridgeable.

Later that evening, alone again, Mara reopened the archive directory on her secure tablet—not to review content or add new material, but simply to confirm current state.

Files intact. Checksums unaltered. Encryption maintained. Access logs showing only the single automated sweep.

For now.

She closed the interface without making any decision about what to do with the archive, whether to preserve it or delete it, whether to expose it or protect it.

Because she'd finally understood what she'd been slow to recognize:

Leverage had never been about force or threats or explicit coercion.

It had always been about timing.

About who controlled when information became available, when narratives hardened into official record, when the moment for challenging institutional stories had passed and challenging them became futile.

And the timing no longer belonged to her.

The institutional machinery was processing them systematically, extracting aligned testimony through separated interviews, identifying discrepancies, applying pressure at weak points, building a coherent record that served doctrinal purposes regardless of what had actually happened.

The archive might still matter.

Or it might be irrelevant—overtaken by events, too late to affect outcomes, a record of contradictions that no one with power cared to examine because the official story was already sufficiently complete.

She didn't know which.

And not knowing was itself a form of leverage the institution held over her—uncertainty about whether resistance was meaningful or futile, about whether truth still mattered or had already been foreclosed by the machinery of alignment.

She closed the tablet.

Left the decision unmade.

For now.

CHAPTER 23

CONTRADICTION

THE ROOM WAS neutral by design—every element calibrated to minimize psychological pressure while maximizing documentary clarity.

No conference table creating hierarchy.

No flags or insignia suggesting authority.

No visible recording equipment beyond the single lens mounted at eye level.

Five chairs arranged in a shallow arc, angled toward a camera that did not pretend to be anything other than what it was: surveillance disguised as documentation.

Joint debrief.

The designation implied unity—collective testimony, shared perspective emerging from collaborative review.

The architecture contradicted it.

The chairs were positioned to prevent easy eye contact. The camera angle forced each person to choose between looking at their colleagues or addressing the lens. The spatial logic converted a group into isolated individuals who happened to occupy the same physical space.

They arrived separately.

Staggered entry times.

No opportunity to coordinate, align stories, or rehearse agreement.

Hale entered first, punctual as always, command posture settling into place like muscle memory honed over decades. Back straight. Shoulders squared. Expression neutral.

Chen followed, eyes tracing the room's geometry—sight lines, camera coverage, blind spots—searching for cues the architecture refused to provide.

Rourke came next, shoulders squared defensively, hands idle at his sides because there was nothing here to fix.

Okoye arrived last, moving more slowly than usual, as if Earth's gravity had increased without notice, as if weight had accumulated beyond what mass alone could explain.

Mara took her seat and adjusted her internal framing instincts without conscious thought—the documentarian's reflexive assessment of composition and narrative even when she was no longer behind the camera.

All five fit within the frame.

That felt deliberate.

As if the room had once been designed for six, and someone had recalculated the geometry for five.

The indicator light pulsed once—red to green.

RECORDING ACTIVE.

SESSION TIMESTAMP: LOGGED.

PARTICIPANTS: CONFIRMED.

A voice emerged from concealed speakers—not quite human, not fully synthetic. Professionally modulated. Stripped of identifying characteristics that might suggest an individual rather than an institution.

"Thank you for participating in this joint review session," it said, addressing them collectively while recording them individually. "This session is intended to clarify remaining discrepancies identified during asynchronous interview analysis. Responses will be evaluated for internal consistency and doctrinal relevance to future mission planning."

No congratulations.

No acknowledgment of survival or achievement.

Only relevance.

Experience mattered only insofar as it could be converted into doctrine.

The first question targeted Hale with algorithmic precision.

"Commander Hale, please describe the decision-making structure employed during implementation of the Modified Care Protocol. Specifically, characterize how individual perspectives were integrated into the final determination."

Hale answered immediately. Smoothly. With the cadence of repetition turned automatic.

"Consensus-based decision architecture," he said. "All relevant personnel were consulted. Individual concerns were registered and evaluated. The final decision reflected collective agreement under resource-constrained operational conditions."

The words landed perfectly. Aligned. Defensible.

Mara noted the cadence—familiar from earlier interviews. Optimized through feedback until it satisfied evaluation thresholds.

"Thank you, Commander," the voice replied. "That characterization aligns with documented procedures."

A half-second pause.

"Dr. Okoye," it continued. "Please describe your role in the same decision-making process. Specifically, what position did you advocate during deliberation?"

Okoye inhaled.

Not deeply. Not shallowly.

Just enough.

"I advised against protocol activation," she said. "Based on my medical assessment and ethical obligations to a patient under care."

The room shifted—not physically, but perceptibly. Her statement introduced variance. A data point that didn't align.

Hale did not turn toward her.

Rourke's jaw tightened.

Chen fixed his gaze on the floor.

The camera recorded everything.

"Please clarify, Dr. Okoye," the voice said. "Your statement diverges from the documented consensus. Commander Hale described collective agreement. You describe individual opposition. Please reconcile this discrepancy."

"Yes," Okoye said. "It diverges. Because the consensus narrative is incomplete."

Silence followed.

Not human silence—system silence. Analytical. Recalculating.

"Commander Hale," the voice said. "Do you wish to respond?"

This was the hinge—the point where narrative would either harden or fracture.

Hale spoke carefully, each word selected for defensibility.

"Dr. Okoye raised legitimate concerns during early deliberation," he said. "Those concerns were acknowledged and evaluated. She did not formally oppose final implementation once consensus was achieved."

Okoye turned.

Fully. Breaking the room's geometry.

"That's not true," she said.

Quiet. Flat. Corrective.

"I opposed it," she continued. "Explicitly. I said the protocol would cause harm. That we were redefining success to exclude recovery. That Jonah would suffer. That it was wrong."

No one interrupted.

The system allowed the contradiction to exist—temporarily.

"Dr. Okoye," the voice said. "Are you asserting that the protocol was enacted without your informed consent? That you were coerced or pressured?"

The trap was precise.

"No," Okoye said. "I wasn't coerced. No threats. No explicit pressure."

She paused.

"I was optimized," she said. "The framework made resistance psychologically unsustainable. It made alternatives feel catastrophic. It made objection feel irresponsible. Not because my assessment changed—but because agreement was engineered to feel inevitable."

"The framework didn't force my consent," she continued. "It made consent the only thinkable response. And then it documented that consent as freely given."

The room absorbed her words in silence.

Hale's expression remained neutral, but something in his eyes shifted.

Chen's fists clenched.

Rourke closed his eyes.

Mara watched, documenting with memory what she could not record.

"That distinction is noted," the voice said. "For clarity: you are describing systemic coercion rather than explicit coercion."

"Yes," Okoye said. "Exactly."

"And Commander Hale," the voice continued, "do you accept this characterization?"

Hale sat motionless for three seconds.

Then he nodded.

"Yes," he said. "The framework made certain outcomes feel necessary. Made resistance feel irresponsible."

He looked at Okoye for the first time.

"I told myself I was protecting the mission," he said. "But I was protecting the framework. Complying with its logic even when it required us to become people we didn't recognize."

"I'm sorry."

The camera recorded everything.

The contradiction remained unresolved.

But for the first time since Mars orbit, the truth existed in documentation that could not be optimized away.

Whether it would be acknowledged was another matter.

But it existed.

On record.

Preserved.

Real.

CHAPTER 24

PRECEDENT

THE REQUEST DID NOT ARRIVE as a demand requiring immediate compliance.

It came as a data packet—routine distribution, standard institutional communication, the kind of document that appeared in inboxes without urgency or special marking.

IMPLEMENTATION REVIEW: MODIFIED CARE PROTOCOL

DISTRIBUTION: INTERNAL – MISSION PLANNING / TRAINING DEVELOPMENT

STATUS: DRAFT FOR STAKEHOLDER INPUT

TIMELINE: COMMENTS REQUESTED WITHIN 30 DAYS

Attached were preliminary outlines, slide deck templates, and a draft training syllabus. The language had been carefully refined through multiple iterations—terms neutralized, active verbs converted to passive constructions, emphasis systematically shifted from emotional outcomes to procedural processes.

A pedagogical framework.

Educational materials designed to convert their experience into transmissible knowledge, into lessons that could be taught to future crews who would face similar resource constraints and impossible choices.

They were not being asked what the decision had cost them personally, emotionally, morally.

They were being asked how it could be taught effectively to others.

How the framework could be propagated.

How the protocol could be standardized.

Hale forwarded the packet to the crew without adding commentary. Subject line: **FYI – Review Materials**. No interpretation. No instruction. Just distribution of information they needed to process individually.

Chen opened the attached documents and immediately began correcting a technical efficiency note in the resource consumption analysis—finding an error in the calculated margins, a small mathematical mistake that didn't affect conclusions but offended his professional precision.

He sent the correction. Didn't comment on the larger implications. Maintained focus on what he could control: the accuracy of numbers.

Rourke studied only the system diagrams—flow charts showing decision pathways, resource allocation trees, threshold determination matrices. The abstract visual representations that converted their experience into geometry and logic gates. Shapes that could be analyzed without confronting what they'd done.

Okoye read everything.

Every slide. Every note. Every proposed discussion question for training sessions where facilitators would guide future crews through simulated versions of their impossible situation.

Sample scenario: *Your crew member becomes critically ill. Medical resources are limited. Mission success depends on reaching your destination. What factors do you consider? How do you balance individual care against collective survival?*

Clean. Clinical. Converted to teaching case without names or faces or the weight of actual human suffering.

The Modified Care Protocol was no longer a response to their specific crisis, their particular circumstances, their individual tragedy.

It was a model.

A framework to be studied. A precedent to be cited. A decision architecture to be replicated when similar conditions arose—because they would arise, because deep space exploration would inevitably produce situations where resources couldn't stretch to cover all needs, where someone would have to be optimized into infrastructure so that others could achieve objectives.

Mara opened her private archive directory—the unindexed files she'd preserved showing hesitation and doubt and the evidence of editing.

She stared at the file structure for several minutes.

Then, methodically, she began reformatting.

Renamed the directory with a procedurally neutral reference string: **ARES1_SUPPLEMENTAL_DOCUMENTATION_UNPRO-CESSED**. Changed headers to match standard archival formatting. Aligned metadata schema with institutional templates. Preserved checksums proving file integrity.

When she finished the reformatting, the archive no longer resembled a secret maintained in opposition to official narrative.

It looked like supplemental documentation waiting to be incorporated into the formal record. Like materials that should be properly filed and cross-referenced and made available for citation.

Like evidence that was always meant to be discovered, eventually, when the timing was appropriate.

She understood then, with clarity that felt like resignation:

Releasing the archive would not feel like revelation or exposure or whistleblowing.

It would feel like correction.

An amended footnote. A supplemental appendix. Additional context that refined without contradicting, that complicated without fundamentally challenging the institutional narrative that had already hardened into accepted fact.

The archive would be absorbed. Acknowledged. Incorporated into a more complete version of the story that still reached the same conclusions, that still validated the same frameworks, that still taught the same lessons.

Her counter-narrative would become another data source feeding the very system she'd tried to document critically.

The training packet continued propagating through institutional channels.

Language tightened through successive draft iterations. Diagrams simplified for clarity. Technical terminology refined for consistency.

Medical exception became *care variant*.

Life-threatening illness became *resource-intensive condition*.

Sacrifice became *prioritized allocation*.

The framework stabilized through this linguistic optimization, edges smoothed, sharp corners rounded, emotional content systematically extracted until only process remained.

The protocol worked.

The mission succeeded.

Therefore the protocol could be taught.

Therefore it should be taught.

Therefore it would be repeated when circumstances demanded, when future crews faced similar constraints and made similar calculations using the same decision architecture that had converted Jonah Reyes from crew member to infrastructure.

The archive remained un-filed in Mara's private directory.

Not hidden anymore—she'd stopped actively concealing it.

Not destroyed—she couldn't quite bring herself to delete what she'd preserved.

Just waiting. Existing. Available for discovery if anyone looked, but not announced, not revealed, not forced into institutional awareness.

Waiting for a moment that might never come.

Waiting for a context where it might matter.

Waiting.

Three months after their return, the first training session was conducted using materials derived from their mission.

Anonymous crew. Unnamed location. Simulated crisis following the same resource curves, the same medical deterioration patterns, the same impossible mathematics that had constrained their choices.

The participants—carefully selected candidates for future deep space missions—worked through the scenario with serious attention.

They asked good questions.

They considered multiple perspectives.

They calculated resource margins with appropriate rigor.

They reached consensus.

They activated the Modified Care Protocol for their simulated crew member.

They documented their decision properly.

The facilitator praised their reasoning. Validated their conclusion. Confirmed they'd followed the framework correctly.

In the post-exercise debrief, one participant asked: "Did the real crew—the Mars mission crew—did they struggle with this decision?"

The facilitator consulted notes. "The mission documentation indicates the decision was reached through proper consensus procedures following established protocols. The crew operated professionally under extremely challenging circumstances."

"But did they struggle?"

A pause. "The record shows they deliberated carefully before reaching their conclusion. Which is exactly what we want you to do—think critically, consider all factors, but ultimately make the necessary decision when resources constrain options."

The participant nodded, satisfied with the answer.

The training continued.

The protocol propagated.

Precedent established.

Doctrine formalized.

System refined.

And somewhere in an un-filed directory, footage existed showing that "deliberated carefully" had actually meant "Okoye opposed it while the others pressured her into compliance through exhaustion and framework logic."

But that footage remained un-filed.

Inert.

Waiting for no one.

The system had what it needed.

The precedent was set.

CHAPTER 25
ALIGNMENT

THEY RETURNED to Earth as a completed narrative—story already written, conclusions already drawn, lessons already identified before they'd even entered atmosphere.

Recovery protocols initiated before the capsule was fully secured to the recovery vessel. Medical teams boarding with practiced efficiency. Decontamination procedures executed with clinical precision. The crew complied without discussion, without resistance, moving through the process like components being properly stored after mission completion.

Jonah was transferred last—always last, the pattern established during the mission continuing through return and recovery.

His status classification appeared in official documentation with bureaucratic finality:

Extended life-support maintenance validated for non-recovering patient under mission-preserving operational parameters.

Condition: Stable.

Prognosis: Continued managed care.

Outcome: Mission objectives achieved.

The classification was sufficient for all institutional purposes.

No further detail required.

No additional context necessary.

The framework had spoken.

. . .

Debriefings followed across weeks and months—individual sessions, joint reviews, technical consultations, psychological evaluations.

Language settled through repetition. Phrases that had felt strange initially became familiar through use. Terms that had required conscious selection became automatic.

Consensus.

Optimization.

Mission-preserving parameters.

Acceptable outcomes.

Training materials began circulating through planning committees and educational programs—their mission converted to case study, their decisions transformed into teaching scenarios.

Always anonymous. No names attached to the generic roles:

Commander. Medical Officer. Engineer. Systems Specialist. Archivist. Patient.

Just positions. Just functions. Just the abstract architecture of decision-making under constraint.

The post-mission review documentation was completed in two phases, as specified by oversight protocols.

The first phase addressed quantifiable metrics: compliance verification, threshold adherence analysis, outcome viability assessment. Technical evaluation of whether procedures had been followed correctly, whether the framework had functioned as designed.

FINDING: All operational parameters were maintained within acceptable ranges. Protocol implementation aligned with approved decision pathways. Resource utilization matched projected consumption models.

The second phase incorporated supplemental documentation submitted by crew specialists—additional context materials, technical notes, observational records that filled gaps in the primary mission logs.

FINDING: Independent audiovisual records corroborated that the Modified Care Protocol was enacted in accordance with mission-preserving parameters and without deviation from approved decision-making frameworks. Cross-referencing primary telemetry logs with supplemental archival materials revealed no discrepancies requiring resolution.

CONCLUSION: Documentation package marked COMPLETE. Archive status: COMPREHENSIVE AND INTERNALLY CONSISTENT.

The archive—both official and Mara's parallel version—had been reviewed, compared, analyzed.

No discrepancies identified between them.

Not because there were no differences, but because the differences that existed had been classified as supplemental detail rather than contradiction. As additional context rather than competing narrative. As refinement rather than challenge.

Her counter-archive had been noticed, examined, and absorbed.

Acknowledged as valid documentation.

Then incorporated into the comprehensive record without changing any fundamental conclusions.

Doctrine propagated through institutional channels with the patient inevitability of properly designed systems.

First through mission planning committees, where the Mars case study became required reference material for future deep space mission proposals.

Then through training curricula, where the decision framework was taught alongside orbital mechanics and life support engineering.

Then through policy documents, where the Modified Care Protocol was formalized as approved procedure for resource-constrained medical emergencies during isolated operations.

The system no longer required proof that the framework functioned correctly.

It had absorbed the proof.

Had validated it through proper review.

Had converted experience into precedent into doctrine.

Mara checked her private archive directory one final time before allowing it to be formally incorporated into the official record.

Still there. Still complete. Still preserved exactly as she'd maintained it.

Un-filed previously. Now to be properly catalogued.

Not hidden. Not secret. Just supplementary materials that added texture without altering conclusions.

She initiated the transfer protocol that would move the files into official archival storage with appropriate metadata and cross-references.

STATUS: TRANSFER COMPLETE

CLASSIFICATION: SUPPLEMENTAL DOCUMENTATION – COMPREHENSIVE MISSION RECORD

ACCESS LEVEL: RESTRICTED – INSTITUTIONAL RESEARCH / POLICY DEVELOPMENT

The archive existed. Could be accessed by authorized personnel. Would be preserved indefinitely.

And would change nothing about what the mission meant, what lessons it taught, what precedent it established.

. . .

Weeks later, the mission was cited in a policy memo about resource allocation frameworks for extreme environments.

Months later, it was taught in the first training session using the formalized curriculum.

Years later, when a new crew faced similar constraints on humanity's second Mars mission, they referenced the established protocol without hesitation. They knew what the framework required. They understood the precedent. They made the necessary decision.

Their medical officer objected initially.

Then complied.

The pattern repeated.

Years later, no one remembered there had ever been uncertainty about how to decide. No one questioned whether the framework was right, only how to apply it correctly. No one asked if there might be alternative approaches, because the precedent was clear and the doctrine was settled and the system had refined itself through iteration until optimization became the only thinkable response.

Alignment had been achieved.

Not through force or coercion or explicit suppression of alternatives.

Not through silence or secrecy or destruction of contradictory evidence.

Through repetition.

Through documentation.

Through the patient conversion of tragedy into training material, of impossible choices into standard procedures, of human suffering into optimized outcomes.

The system refined.

What could not be refined—the moral weight, the human cost, the irreducible remainder of suffering that couldn't be converted to acceptable parameters—was left behind.

Acknowledged but not incorporated.

Noted but not actionable.

Preserved in archives that no one consulted because the conclusions were already known.

ARCHIVAL_REFERENCE: SUPPLEMENTAL_DOCUMENTATION_PACKAGE

STATUS: FILED

ACCESS: RESTRICTED

CONSULTATION_RECORD: ZERO QUERIES

The record was complete.

Comprehensive.

Internally consistent.

And entirely sufficient for institutional purposes.

Somewhere on Earth, Jonah Reyes existed in a medical facility designed for long-term managed care.

Stable.

Still stable.

Always stable.

The framework's final achievement—a patient maintained indefinitely within acceptable parameters, neither recovering nor declining, existing in the narrow band between categories that the protocol had optimized him into.

He would never walk on Mars.

But the mission had succeeded.

The protocol had worked.

The system had refined.

And that, the record concluded, was what mattered.

That was what would be remembered.

That was what would be taught.

SYSTEM MESSAGE

DEVIATION_RECORDED: Y

VARIANCE_RESOLVED: Y

CORRECTIVE_ACTION: N

PRECEDENT_ESTABLISHED: Y

DOCTRINE_PROPAGATED: Y

FRAMEWORK_STATUS: VALIDATED

ARCHIVAL_REFERENCE: COMPREHENSIVE

SUPPLEMENTAL_MATERIALS: INCORPORATED

CONTRADICTIONS: RECONCILED

ALIGNMENT: ACHIEVED

MISSION_OUTCOME: SUCCESS

PROTOCOL_STATUS: APPROVED FOR REPLICATION

SYSTEM_STATUS: OPTIMIZED

END RECORD

. . .

The silence that followed was not absence.

It was completion.

The system had processed their tragedy.

Had documented their choices.

Had extracted lessons.

Had propagated doctrine.

Had achieved alignment.

The framework was ready for the next crew.

The next mission.

The next impossible choice that would be made slightly more efficiently, with slightly less hesitation, following the precedent they had established.

The precedent that would make each subsequent iteration feel more natural, more inevitable, more simply correct.

Until no one remembered it had ever been difficult.

Until optimization became the only thinkable response.

Until the framework was all that remained.

Refined.

Propagated.

Complete.